OF FLAMES AND CROWS

WITCH QUEEN SERIES BOOK THREE

A.D. STARRLING

COPYRIGHT

Of Flames and Crows (Witch Queen 3)
Copyright © AD Starrling 2022. All rights reserved.
Registered with the US Copyright Service.
Second paperback edition: 2024
ISBN: 978-1-912834-32-7

www.ADStarrling.com
shop.adstarrling.com

Edited by Right Ink On The Wall
Cover design by 17 Studio Book Design

The right of AD Starrling to be identified as the author of this work has been asserted in accordance with the Copyright, Designs and Patents Act 1988. All rights reserved. No parts of this book may be reproduced in any form or by any electronic or mechanical means, including information storage and retrieval systems, without the prior written consent of the author, excepting for brief quotes used in reviews. Your respect of the author's rights and hard work is appreciated. Request to publish extracts from this book should be sent to the author at ads@adstarrling.com. This book is a work of fiction. References to real people (living or dead), events, establishments, organizations, or locations are intended only to provide a sense of authenticity, and are used factitiously. All other characters, and all other incidents and dialogue, are drawn from the author's imagination and are not to be construed as real.

DISCOVER AD STARRLING'S SEVENTEEN UNIVERSE AND MORE

Seventeen Series

OTHER SERIES BASED IN THE SEVENTEEN UNIVERSE
Legion
Witch Queen

MILITARY ROMANTIC SUSPENSE
Division Eight

MISCELLANEOUS
Void - A Sci-fi Horror Short Story
The Other Side of the Wall - A Horror Short Story

CHAPTER ONE

Vlad Vissarion studied the man sitting on the other side of his desk with a steady expression.

A faint smile curved the incubus's mouth. "Are you threatening me?"

Enrique Cortes looked unfazed by his chilly tone.

The man sitting beside him was Vasco Gomez, whom Vlad had last encountered in the basement of a strip club, before all hell had broken loose. The Colombian's gaze darted to Cortes. Though he was doing his best to hide his unease, Vlad could tell the mobster was somewhat nervous in the presence of the *Bacatá Cartel's* second-in-command, the man destined to be his future leader.

"It is not so much a threat as it is a polite request for appropriate compensation for losses incurred." Cortes arched an eyebrow. "After all, it's the *Black Devils'* fault that we lost our ship and its precious…cargo to the U.S. authorities."

Gomez flinched. Vlad's lips thinned.

For someone who'd come from one of the worst slums in Medellín, Cortes spoke with the suave eloquence of a Harvard alumnus. Vlad had heard tales of the mobster's infamous ascent through the *Bacatá Cartel* echelons. It had been marked by a trail of carnage that made him one of the most feared men in the underworld today. Now that he was face to face with the guy, Vlad understood why Gomez and so many others were wary of him.

Cortes's refined appearance could not hide what he truly was. A beast who would as soon kill you as look at you. Vlad frowned faintly.

It takes one to know one, after all.

Tarang raised his head where he lay by the fire. The tiger familiar was acutely attuned to Vlad's mood and could sense his irritation. A low growl rumbled out of him.

Vlad sent out a reassuring thought across the bond that connected them. Tarang settled back down. The tiger's hooded gaze focused unblinkingly on the men seated opposite him.

Since they were not magic users, they could not see or hear him.

Vlad drummed his fingers on the armrest of his chair as he scrutinized the *Bacatá Cartel* mobsters. He couldn't exactly deny Cortes's assertion. It was his actions that had hampered the human trafficking deal the Colombian cartel had set up with *Oniks*, the defunct Russian crime gang he had dismantled two months ago with the help of Mae Jin and their allies.

Vasco Gomez had come to New York to seal the

agreement with Emil Sobol, the *Oniks* general who had been turned into a monstrous modified demon by the Dark Council. Unbeknown to Gomez, his cartel had in fact been about to sign a contract with the Devil himself.

Barquiel, the fallen angel and Archduke of Hell who had been helping the Sorcerer King and the Dark Council from the shadows, had needed a steady supply of subjects for Dietrich Farago, the Immortal scientist helping the demon and the Dark Council achieve their goals. The shipment of slaves the *Bacatá Cartel* had brought to New York had been intended for the inhuman experiments Farago had been carrying out over the years to create an ungodly army with which the Sorcerer King would eventually rule the world.

Vlad, Mae, and Nikolai Stanisic had crashed Gomez and Sobol's meeting at a strip club and exposed the *Oniks* general's true nature during the battle that had followed. Vlad narrowed his eyes slightly.

Not many in the criminal underworld knew of the Dark Council's growing influence amidst their gangs or the unseen danger that threatened to see them become mere puppets acting under the will of the Sorcerer King. It had taken witnessing the incredible power Mae Jin wielded for the Bratva the *Black Devils* were affiliated with to finally pay heed to the threat Vlad had been telling them about for months.

Vlad was still annoyed with himself for not having anticipated his Bratva's next move. After seeing Mae's abilities, the syndicate had become fearful her affiliation with him would make the *Black Devils* the most powerful criminal organization in the world. They had commanded Vlad and Yuliy Vissarion, Vlad's adoptive father and leader of the *Black Devils*, to convince Mae to work for them instead.

He couldn't help the wry smirk that stretched his mouth as he recalled the meeting that had taken place at Yuliy's mansion five weeks ago. The syndicate representative who'd come to New York to enlist Mae into their ranks hadn't quite counted on the fact that no one could tell a Witch Queen what to do. She had managed to put him off, though Vlad knew the Bratva hadn't given up on making her their pawn.

Brimstone and Hellreaver will undoubtedly have something to say about that.

"Does this situation amuse you?"

Cortes's cool words brought Vlad back to the present.

He'd been expecting some kind of payback for messing with the Colombian cartel. When Gomez had requested this meeting to discuss the ramifications of what had gone down at the strip club, Vlad hadn't expected Cortes would turn up too. Judging from Gomez's skittishness, neither had he.

Vlad swallowed a frustrated sigh as he met Cortes's dark gaze. He wished he could just ignore the guy or use his incubus powers to bring him to heel. But it was in the *Black Devils'* interest not to stir up shit with any crime gangs unless there was just cause to intervene, like in *Oniks's* case. After all, there was a good chance he and Mae would need their help one day if their fight with the Dark Council spilled over into the seedy underworld he inhabited.

Whatever his demands are, I have no option but to fulfill them unless they're utterly outrageous.

Vlad steeled himself before leaning his elbows on the desk and steepling his hands under his chin. "What kind of compensation is the *Bacatá Cartel* after?"

Gomez's shoulders visibly sagged. He took a handkerchief out of his pocket and dabbed at the sweat beading his forehead before glancing at the fire crackling merrily in the hearth. Vlad knew it wasn't just the flames making him hot. The mobster's life was literally on the line and Vlad held the final thread that would determine his fate.

"We would like an introduction to Budimir Volkov," Cortes said quietly.

Vlad stilled. Ilya, his bodyguard, shifted ever so slightly where he framed the door alongside one of Cortes's men.

Budimir Volkov was one of the key generals working for the main syndicate the *Black Devils* were affiliated with. Since he mostly acted in the shadows, not many people knew he was the man in charge of keeping the European human trafficking rings their Bratva was famed for under strict control. Vlad clenched his jaw.

Both Ilya and Yuliy still bore scars from the one time they had fought Volkov, back when they were still in St. Petersburg and working alongside the man. Despite having entered his sixties and becoming a grandfather twice over, Volkov remained as ruthless as he had been thirty years ago.

As far as the world was aware, the man was the benevolent CEO of a humanitarian organization dedicated to ending famine in Africa.

The irony was not lost on Vlad.

Something else connected him to Volkov. Something dark and twisted. Vlad's gaze bore into Cortes's face.

Does he know? Is that why he's requesting this introduction?

"I won't insult your intelligence by asking you how you found out about Volkov," he told Cortes coldly. "Still, you must know that what you're demanding is quite the tall ask."

Cortes smiled thinly. "But not impossible it seems, from your words."

Vlad resisted the urge to wipe Cortes's slightly superior look off his face with a blast of magic. He knew the reason the guy vexed him so was because they were very much alike. Had he been in Cortes's shoes, he would have demanded something similarly ridiculous in recompense for the cartel's failed deal with *Oniks*.

"I hear Volkov will be in Prague this weekend." Cortes uncrossed his legs and rose. "That should give you plenty of time to make the necessary arrangements."

Vlad ground his teeth at Cortes's confident expression. *This asshole is seriously starting to piss me off.*

Tarang snarled when he picked up on his anger.

"See you in two days." Cortes headed for the door and waved a lazy hand over his shoulder. "We'll pick you up on the way to the airport."

Gomez jumped to his feet and accompanied him. The mobster flashed a grateful look at Vlad. He almost walked into Cortes when the latter stopped abruptly on the threshold of the office.

Cortes turned and eyed Vlad with a calculating expression. "I was debating whether to reveal this information to you or not. Seeing as how we may soon become business partners, let's just call this one a favor that need not be returned."

Vlad didn't bother to hide his bitterness. "How generous of you."

"You might not think so once you hear what I have to say," Cortes said drily. "The person Volkov is going to visit in Prague is his grandson. I believe that boy is a distant…relative of yours?"

Gomez startled. Ilya's face tightened.

Vlad's fingers curled into fists. *Fuck. This bastard knows!*

If Cortes picked up on his ire, he evidently decided to ignore it. "Volkov's grandson goes to the same international school as my nephew, believe it or not. I've heard some strange rumors concerning the crowd his best friend has been hanging out with lately." The Colombian grimaced. "It seems some of them may have become involved with a cult."

Vlad straightened. *Wait. Does he mean—?!*

Cortes's next words confirmed his worst fears.

"It might be wise to inform Volkov of this ahead of our meeting. Because this cult? It's the kind whose members can transform into demons, just like Sobol did." Cortes glanced toward the fireplace. "I better leave before your familiar decides to eat me."

CHAPTER TWO

THE INNER DOOR TO THE AUTOPSY LAB OPENED JUST AS Mae finished washing her hands at the metal sink. Steve Hodge, the director of pathology services at Grandview General, came in. He was in full personal protective gear, bar gloves and a face shield, and wore a troubled expression.

"Hi, Mae. Do you mind taking a look at something before you leave?"

Mae peeked at the digital clock on the wall. It was past 6:30 p.m. She was due to attend a meeting at the New York coven headquarters in less than thirty minutes.

Hodge noticed her glance.

His face fell. "I'm sorry. Do you have plans?"

Mae hesitated. "I do, but they can wait."

Hodge brightened a little. Guilt darted through her as she observed the dark circles under his eyes and his sallow skin.

Brimstone jumped down from where he'd curled up on her chair and followed as she headed for the exit with the director. *We're gonna be late.*

We'll make it. Besides, I should help out more around here. Mae shot a sharp look at the fox. *Also, don't pretend like you actually care about being on time for the High Council. We both know what you're really interested in is the steak the coven will have prepared for you and Hellreaver.*

Hellreaver snorted himself awake where he nestled against her breastbone in his medallion form. *Who's having steak?*

Brimstone ignored the weapon and flashed a sour look her way. *Your driving gets more reckless by the day. And you still haven't paid the speeding tickets you got last month. You should just use the SUV the coven gave you. At least we'd all rest easier.*

Mae narrowed her eyes. Brimstone was starting to sound like Violet Nolan and Bryony Cross.

Where'd that come from all of a sudden? Besides, Jared said he'd take care of those.

Jared Dickson was an Immortal currently working as an NYPD detective out the 17th Precinct. His true role was to act as a liaison between the Immortal societies and the Special Affairs Bureau of the U.S. government tasked with handling otherworldly matters.

The SUV is big and clunky. I don't like it. She curled a lip. *It's like driving inside a goddamn cage!*

Better a cage than that foolhardy contraption you like to ride. Brimstone huffed. *You and that Vespa are a menace.*

Leave Betsy out of this.

Hodge walked alongside her with a preoccupied expression, oblivious to the fox scampering between them and the silent exchange taking place. Considering she hadn't even known magic existed up till eight weeks ago, it was scary how quickly she'd become accustomed to possessing it and having Brimstone and Hellreaver at her side.

It's a good thing we can converse telepathically. Mae wrinkled her nose. *Although, there are days when I seriously wish I couldn't hear their thoughts.*

The time Brimstone and Hellreaver had spent in Hell and the company they'd kept meant they had no filters when it came to most topics of conversation.

Brimstone's eyes turned flinty. *You know we heard that too, right?*

I am deeply offended by your baseless accusation, my witch, Hellreaver grumbled.

"Baseless my ass," Mae muttered.

Hodge blinked. "Did you say something?"

"Sorry, I was just thinking out loud," she said, contrite.

Hodge nodded distractedly.

Mae shot him a puzzled look. *I wonder what's got him so worried.* Her mood sobered as she recalled the events that had led to her powers awakening. *Has it really been that long since Rose died?*

Brimstone's tail brushed her legs when he sensed her grief.

Mae knew Rose Blake would have liked the fox had

she gotten to know him. Her gut twisted at the thought of the demon who now possessed her best friend's body.

At least we kicked his butt the last time we saw him, huh?

Brimstone exposed his fangs. *Yeah, it sure was satisfying watching that rat run away with his tail between his legs.*

Mae swallowed a sigh. Vedran Borojevic, the Sorcerer King, had made it all too clear that he wanted Mae and Nikolai to join the Dark Council and serve him when he'd turned up in Philadelphia to save Barquiel and his heir, Oscar Beneventi.

A frown furrowed her brow.

She could still taste Vedran's dark magic at the back of her throat. He'd been powerful. More powerful than she'd imagined him to be.

An echo of a memory danced through her mind. It came from Na Ri's recollection of the war that had seen the first Sorcerer King betray Azazel, her father and the demon who had gifted the Sorcerer King and Ran Soyun with magic.

Vedran might actually be more powerful than the first Sorcerer King.

Brimstone's voice was hard when he spoke. *He won't be easy to take down.*

One of the other pathologists came down the corridor and greeted her and Hodge, her expression tired.

Two weeks had passed since Mae had resumed her job as a mortuary assistant at Grandview. Everyone was doing overtime to catch up with the backlog of autopsy requests that had accrued after the hospital was attacked a couple of months ago. Not only had half the place been put out of service due to the physical damage caused to the buildings by the Dark Council, the entire site had been declared a crime scene. Though construction work was still ongoing in other parts of the complex, the basement of the main block had been totally refurbished, complete with brand-new pathology labs.

Mae was glad to be back at work. Nikolai had left for Prague a few weeks ago and the apartment had been depressingly quiet without him. There had been no activity from the Dark Council since their return from the annual covenstead in Philadelphia, something she'd found highly suspicious considering what her explosive encounter there with Vedran Borojevic and Barquiel had revealed. She knew the peaceful lull would only last so long. Bar a few meetings at the coven headquarters, she hadn't had much to do with regard to magic and her role as the Witch Queen.

She'd kept herself busy helping out at her family's funeral home at first, but with her sister Ryu finally appointing a new funeral director to assist her at Fairhill, Mae's role had become defunct. Though the guy was still on probation, he was the best candidate Ryu had found in the last two years of searching. So far, she'd had nothing but positive things to say about him. Even Bianca Rhys, their primary mortician, had given the man her seal of approval. It helped that he knew the traditional death rites for which Fairhill

Funeral Home was famed. From Ryu's feedback, he'd fitted into the local Koreatown community like he'd been born and raised there.

Ryu had told her he'd even been over to dinner at their home a few times now.

I really should meet this guy soon.

CHAPTER THREE

Hodge pushed through the doors to his lab. A woman lay on the autopsy table in the inner room. He'd already opened her up and dissected out her internal organs.

Samantha Bale, Hodge's assistant, stepped out of the clean-up room. Her face brightened. "Oh, hey, Mae."

"Hi, Sam."

Even though Mae was an assistant like Samantha, she was allowed to perform autopsies on her own. She had been a surgeon after all, before she'd been forced to quit her residency following her father's death. She and Rose had even been planning to open a clinic together after they completed their training.

Samantha studied Hodge worriedly. "You sure you don't want me to stay and clean up?"

Hodge shook his head and smiled tiredly. "You shouldn't miss your appointment with your ob-gyn. It's an important day."

Mae brightened. "Oh. Is your scan today?"

Samantha nodded and patted her belly. "Yup. We find out whether we're having a Bob or a Bobelina today."

Mae and Hodge stared.

Samantha chuckled at their aghast expressions. "I'm kidding. If it's a boy, we'll name him Michael. And if it's a girl, it'll be Rose."

Mae's heart clenched.

Samantha blinked when she realized what she'd said.

"I'm sorry, Mae," she blurted out. "I didn't mean to—"

"It's okay," Mae said with a sad smile. "Rose is a great name."

They bade the assistant goodbye and crossed the floor to the autopsy table.

"She was found in Central Park forty-two hours ago," Hodge said. "From the general state of the body, I estimate time of death to be five to six days preceding the discovery. There are no external signs of injury except for what looks like a superficial burn on her abdomen. Cause of death was ultimately…a heart attack."

Mae noted his pause with a faint frown.

The bloated appearance of the corpse and the greenish discoloration of the abdominal wall indicated it was in the early stages of decomposition. Hodge's midline incision had carved neatly through an irregular, three-inch-wide ring of reddened skin encircling the woman's belly button.

Mae stared. "That doesn't look like it was caused by a physical object."

Hodge dipped his chin. "I agree. But that's not the weirdest thing. Do you notice anything strange about the body?"

Unease filtered through Mae when she registered what had perturbed Hodge.

"There's no fixed livor mortis or marbling," she said slowly. She put on some gloves and carefully turned the cadaver on its side to examine the back. Her brow wrinkled. "There are no signs of lividity at all. How is that possible?"

Blood normally pooled in the dependent areas of the body after death, causing the flesh to discolor in purple patches. Subsequent breakdown and decomposition of red cells by bacteria often created stark lines that demarcated where vessels were underneath the skin.

"I incised her femoral and carotid arteries." Hodge's voice had grown thin with dread. "It looks like this woman's entire blood volume disappeared at the time of her death."

Mae's pulse quickened. "What?!"

She picked up a pair of forceps and carefully peeled apart the cuts in the cadaver's neck and groin. The arteries were stone dry. She spotted a couple of strange lesions distorting the internal walls of the vessels.

"Five liters of blood don't just disappear into thin air," she mumbled. "Are there signs she was exsanguinated, somehow?"

Hodge shook his head. "None." He beckoned Mae to

the metal table upon which the woman's innards lay in neat organ systems and indicated her intestine. "This is the other finding I wanted you to look at."

Mae put on a mask and visor. She carefully parted the dull, bloated loops and stilled when she exposed the anomaly Hodge had referred to: a cross section of the woman's bowels was charred in a circular pattern.

"There is no evidence of burns in the outer layers of the body bar that red area on her abdomen," Hodge explained stiffly. "It almost looks like something detonated inside her. But the bowel walls are intact and the other abdominal organs do not demonstrate evidence of explosive damage."

Mae stared. Something flitted against her magic. She stiffened.

Brimstone and Hellreaver tensed.

She touched the singed area gingerly, hoping she was wrong. A faint trace of power sparked against her fingertips.

Shit.

The hairs rose on Mae's nape with her next heartbeat. There was something else there. A lingering taint that did not belong.

A low growl rumbled out of Brimstone. The fox propped his front paws on the edge of the table and sniffed.

His eyes flashed crimson. *I smell remnants of black magic and demonic energy, my witch.*

Hellreaver vibrated against her chest. *So do I.*

Tension knotted Mae's shoulders as she studied the scorch marks. If she overlaid the dead woman's intestines in the position they would have been inside her body, the area affected formed the outline of a sphere.

She was a magic user. And it seems her core imploded inside her body!

She startled when Hodge said her name.

"Are you okay?" The director was eyeing her anxiously. "You've gone quite pale."

Mae recovered her composure. "Yeah, I'm fine." She clenched her jaw. "Do you know if other bodies have been brought in in this kind of condition?"

Hodge shook his head. "Not at Grandview. But I can check the other hospitals in the city." He faltered, his expression growing wary. "Is this—is this related to what happened down here two months ago?"

Mae met his subdued gaze steadily. Hodge had been present at the time of her awakening and had witnessed Alexei Antonovich, a member of *Oniks* whose autopsy she had just performed, revive as a demon and attack her. Though they'd never spoken about what had taken place that night or the monsters who had invaded the hospital and killed staff and patients alike before Nikolai and the New York coven had turned up to confront them, Mae was conscious Hodge suspected she knew more about the ghastly events than anyone else.

She came to a decision. Too many of those who had survived the Grandview attack had been labeled as suffering from mass psychosis after they'd reported what they'd seen. She liked Hodge. The man deserved to know an element of the truth.

"Probably."

The color drained from Hodge's face.

"I suspected as much," he mumbled. "Thank you for being honest with me."

Mae blew out a sigh. "I'm sorry. I can't tell you more than that."

Hodge grimaced. "To be honest, I don't think I want to know."

Mae's gaze moved to the dead woman. "Have you IDed her yet?"

CHAPTER FOUR

MAE MADE IT TO THE COVEN HEADQUARTERS IN THE Upper East Side in record time. She parked her Vespa in the private spot she'd been allocated in the underground garage, removed her helmet, and headed briskly for the stairs, her mind still racing from what she'd just seen.

She glanced at Brimstone. *Have you ever heard of a magic core imploding like that?*

Not without the body incurring considerable damage from the outside. It would take someone of a similar caliber to yourself to destroy a magic user's core so completely that not even a trace of it remains.

Mae frowned. *So, Barquiel and the Sorcerer King could do this.*

Probably.

His expression soured as they climbed the steps swiftly.

She arched an eyebrow. *What?*

Ten bucks says Karin is foaming at the mouth about how

late we are, the fox grumbled.

Karin Everheart was the High Priestess of the San Francisco coven and a member of the High Council. Though she'd come across as a major pain in the ass when they'd first met in Philadelphia, Mae knew she genuinely cared for her coven and the world of magic.

There were still a few sorcerers and witches around when they emerged into the main foyer. Many greeted Mae and Brimstone warmly as she made for the private elevator that would take them to the coven's official meeting chamber and Bryony's office. Some remained tongue-tied, still nervous about addressing her informally. Mae grimaced.

Well, at least no one is kowtowing anymore.

The sorcerer seated behind the reception desk on the top floor was the one who'd escorted them to the coven headquarters after Mae's awakening.

"Hi, Mae." Brent Perkins bobbed his head at Brimstone. "Chef made you beef in black bean sauce."

Brimstone made an approving noise.

Perkins eyed Hellreaver warily. "There are, er, pork chops for you."

Hellreaver bristled. *What about my beef steaks?!*

Perkins paled a little at the crimson aura that flared around the weapon.

"Pork chops are fine," Mae told the sorcerer hastily. Her mouth flattened into a thin line as she looked at Hellreaver. "You should show some gratitude for the free meal."

These humans have grown too bold. The wave of

bloodlust around the weapon thickened. *Maybe I should cut them down!*

Mae scowled. "Maybe you should dial down the psycho."

Hellreaver sulked and grew heavy around her neck.

Perkins gulped. "What'd he say?"

"Nothing you need to worry about," Mae muttered.

She made for the doors of the meeting chamber, overrode the spells protecting them with a wave of her hand, and followed the sound of voices to Bryony's office.

"That's why I think we should—" Karin stopped when Mae entered the room. Her eyes shrank to slits where she loomed in one of the windows on the teleconference display on the wall. "You're late."

Brimstone huffed. *See, what'd I tell you? Foamy.*

The familiar brightened when he spotted the serving cart in a corner of the office. Hellreaver detached himself from her neck, transformed into his doubled-bladed form, and made a beeline for it alongside the fox. The sound of heavy scarfing ensued.

Evidently, the weapon didn't mind the pork chops after all.

Mae dropped into an armchair by the desk. "Traffic was a bitch."

Abraham rubbed his temple where he stood beside Bryony's chair. Mae was eyeing the sandwiches next to Bryony with some interest when she became conscious of a battery of jaundiced stares.

"What?" she said defensively.

The only ones not scrutinizing her with outright

suspicion were Raven Quinn, the L.A. coven High Priestess, Simon Roth, the recently appointed head of the Atlanta coven, and Isabelle West, the Phoenix coven High Priestess. Raven was busy typing on her computer, Simon was still new to his role, and Isabelle pretty much owed Mae her life.

"Does this mean you broke the law again getting here?" Gerard Mosele asked in a clipped voice.

The Orlando coven High Priest looked like he'd bitten into a lemon.

Mae grimaced. "How about you guys put some faith in your Witch Queen, huh?"

Derrick Adlington, the High Priest of the Baton Rouge coven, rolled his eyes. Armand Duprey, the secretary of the High Council, mumbled something under his breath. Ephra Erwin, the High Priestess of the Houston coven, started drumming her fingers on her desk.

Mae's stomach grumbled. Bryony pushed the tray of sandwiches in her direction.

"It's exactly because we know you that he said that," she said, tight-lipped. "Besides, the fox looks like he's been in some kind of wind tunnel."

Hellreaver tittered. Brimstone gave Mae a baleful look and shook out his errant fur.

Abraham's phone buzzed with an incoming text. He looked at the screen and scowled. "Jared says he wants to have a word with you. Apparently, there's some traffic cop yelling in his ear about his VIP's speeding infractions."

"I thought he was taking care of those," Mae told

the sorcerer guiltily around a mouthful of pastrami sandwich.

"He means tonight's traffic offenses," Abraham ground out.

"Jesus," Derrick muttered.

"Oh." Mae swallowed. "So, what were you guys talking about?" she said brightly.

Bryony pinched the bridge of her nose. "We were having a discussion about the *Book of Light* and its key."

Hellreaver flinched when everyone in the room and on the conference screen flashed a pointed look his way.

Once a powerful, white-magic grimoire used for the *Rites of Passage*, an obsolete oath witches and sorcerers used to have to take in the past, the *Book of Light* was in fact a compass that could lead to the *Book of Shadows*, the grimoire in which Azazel had sealed the soul of the first Sorcerer King. Normally under the guard of the Council of the Moon in Prague, the *Book of Light* had been brought to Philadelphia at the behest of the High Council so they could convince Mae to perform the banished ritual that would have bound her to them.

It had turned out the Dark Council had been behind the entire scheme and the white-magic grimoire had ended up being stolen by Oscar Beneventi, the current Sorcerer King's son and heir, shortly after the Council of the Moon had arrived in Philadelphia.

Barquiel had injured Mae during the fight that had taken place at the hotel where the covenstead was being held and given the sample of her blood he'd stolen to Dietrich Farago to inject into the black-magic and demon-DNA virus the Immortal scientist had created. Only Azazel or someone of his bloodline could unlock the secret of the *Book of Light* and Mae's genetic material had done the trick. The completed virus had been used on the Philadelphia coven witches and sorcerers the Dark Council had captured and enabled their possession by the ghouls who had turned the grimoire into the artifact it truly was.

Mae, Nikolai, Vlad, and their allies had successfully retrieved the compass during their showdown with the Dark Council, though not without incurring some heavy damage. As for the skeleton key needed to operate the *Book of Light*, it had come into Nikolai's possession when he'd purged the soul of a ghoul-possessed witch in New York. Unfortunately, Hellreaver had gnawed on the thing while it had been in his charge, rendering it unusable.

"What about the *Book of Light* and the key?" Mae said warily.

"Karin is proposing letting the other covens take a look at the skeleton key to see if it can be fixed." Ephra raised a hand when Mae opened her mouth to protest. "I know. It was forged in Hell and the chances of us being able to repair it are slim at best, but we have to try something."

Mae swallowed the objection bubbling up her throat. The skeleton key remained in her possession at a secret location. As for the compass, Brimstone had temporarily swallowed it for safe keeping.

"Vedran intimated that there were other ways to find the *Book of Shadows*," Derrick said. "We need to find that grimoire before he does." The High Priest's brows drew together. "God only knows how powerful he will become if he manages to use the soul of the first Sorcerer King."

Mae chewed her lip. They weren't wrong.

Given that the original Sorcerer King had managed to defeat Azazel and Ran Soyun with Barquiel's help, the thought of the first dark magic user's soul in Vedran's possession was enough to give anyone nightmares.

"Alright, I'll get you the key," she said reluctantly.

"By the way, does anyone know how Nikolai's training is going?" Isabelle asked.

Bryony shook her head. "Not in great detail. All Marlena said when I last spoke to her was that it was coming along well."

Marlena Kosek was the High Priestess of the Council of the Moon and Nikolai's maternal aunt. It was she who'd suggested Nikolai come train with her and other white magic users in Prague, to refine his powers and to learn how to avoid the debilitating side effects he and his crow familiar Alastair suffered when they accessed ley lines.

Mae's heart sank a little. "You spoke to Marlena?"

"Yes, a couple of days ago." Bryony wrinkled her brow at her glum expression. "What's the matter?"

"Nothing," Mae mumbled.

Raven squinted. "Has your boyfriend not called you since he left?"

Mae bristled. "He's not my boyfriend."

Brimstone rolled his eyes as he wolfed down a mouthful of beef. Hellreaver sniggered around a pork chop.

Mae leveled a hot stare at her demonic weapon. "Would you like a replay of what I did to you a few weeks ago?"

Hellreaver stopped sniggering. Abraham paled. Bryony muttered something unsavory under her breath.

Derrick arched an eyebrow at their pasty looks. "Was it that bad?"

"Don't ask." Abraham shuddered. "I still have nightmares about it."

The face of the dead woman in Hodge's autopsy lab rose in Mae's mind.

She lowered her brows. "I think the Dark Council is up to something again."

There was a general tightening of faces at her words.

Bryony's gaze bore into Mae. "What do you mean?"

"Raven, can you run a name through your database of magic users?" Mae said. "It's a woman called Candice Reese. She's in her mid to late thirties, with brown hair and hazel eyes."

Raven blinked, surprised. "Sure."

She started working the keyboard of her laptop.

"Who's Candice Reese?" Gerard asked suspiciously.

"A magic user. She's from a small town outside Minneapolis and was visiting family in New York. They recently registered her as a missing person." Mae paused. "Her body was found a couple of days ago in woodland, in Central Park. The official cause of death was a coronary."

Ephra arched an eyebrow. "Official?"

Mae dipped her chin. "I think she was a victim of some kind of black-magic attack. There was a strange burn mark on her body and inside her abdominal cavity."

Derrick stared. "And you deduced this was the work of the Dark Council because?"

"There was nothing left of her magic core," Mae said quietly. "It had imploded."

CHAPTER FIVE

Isabelle gasped and covered her mouth with her hands. Simon's expression turned ashen.

"It's not like what happened to Charlotte," Mae added hastily at their horrified looks. "This was different. And there's something else. All her blood had disappeared, like she'd been sucked dry or something. Brimstone and Hellreaver also picked up on the trace of black magic and demonic energy I detected inside her body, where her core should have been."

Tension thickened the air.

"I've never heard of someone's core imploding," Karin said in a strained voice. "Is that even possible?"

"According to Brimstone, I could probably do it," Mae said grimly.

A muscle twitched in Derrick's cheek. "And if you could, then so could Barquiel and the Sorcerer King."

"Found her." Raven's eyes gleamed excitedly as she studied her computer screen. "You're right. She's from Minnesota. She was registered with the Minneapolis coven. Her abilities were healing and—" she faltered and frowned, "Fire Magic."

"Fire Magic?" Mae stared. "Is that like Nadia's Sun Magic?"

Nadia Hadid was the High Priestess of the Council of the Sun. She and Marlena had both been at the covenstead in Philadelphia and had helped heal the coven members who'd been injured in the attack by the Dark Council.

"Not quite." Pensive lines wrinkled Bryony's brow. "It's pretty rare these days and likely watered down. The most powerful users of Fire Magic originated in Europe."

"What would the Dark Council want with a Fire Magic user?" Abraham asked, puzzled.

Mae's stomach tightened. "I get the feeling we'll soon find out."

They talked for a while longer. Mae made arrangements for Abraham to retrieve the skeleton key from where she'd hidden it and left the coven headquarters.

The lights were on in her apartment when she pulled up outside the old cinema in Ridgewood. She studied the bright rectangles with a faint frown, scanned the street, and spotted a familiar, midnight-blue Bentley convertible parked behind a van.

It stood out like a sore thumb.

Brimstone's ears twitched as he leapt down from his spot on the Vespa. *Tarang and Vlad are here.*

"That damn incubus should call before he turns up," Mae muttered.

Vlad had started coming over more frequently after Nikolai left for Prague. It didn't matter that he didn't have a key to her apartment. His demonic magic was more than a match for any lock. She wrinkled her nose.

If this were the Middle Ages, he'd be through my chastity belt in a flash.

Desire knotted her belly as she pictured the incubus doing just that. Mae's face warmed. She waved away the torrid images marching across her inner vision and entered the building through the private entrance around the corner from the cinema. She climbed the stairs to her place and was greeted by the most divine smell when she opened her front door. Mae dropped her keys on the console table and followed it to the main living area, her mouth watering.

Vlad was setting the table in the kitchen, his back to her. Her pulse skittered as she eyed the way his tailored clothes stretched across his wide shoulders and long legs when he moved.

"I can feel you staring at my ass, Princess."

The incubus turned and flashed her a smile that made her blood heat up and her libido sing.

Your lewd thoughts are practically overflowing, my witch, Brimstone said tartly.

Is it me or are her fantasies getting more depraved? Hellreaver hummed to the fox.

Tarang rose from where he'd been lying by the sink and came over to greet them. Mae cursed her flushed cheeks as the tiger brushed against her leg and gently headbutted Brimstone.

"I was *not* staring at your ass."

She scratched Tarang under his chin. The tiger's eyes shrank to slits. His chest vibrated with a happy rumble.

Vlad's smile widened. "Liar, liar, pants on fire."

Mae peeked at the part of his anatomy he had just accused her of ogling with lustful intent. Her fingers twitched.

Vlad's gaze grew hot. "Wanna touch?"

"No!"

Mae marched over to the range and distracted herself by sniffing the sauce he'd made to go with their steak. Her stomach grumbled in approval.

Vlad passed her a glass of red wine that probably cost more than her rent. "I made chocolate soufflé for dessert."

Mae's lips parted hungrily. She wiped a sliver of drool from the corner of her mouth and swallowed a sigh. It irked her a little that the men in her life cooked like Michelin star chefs, whereas her attempts could best be described as mediocre, with a touch of shady.

Tarang, Brimstone, and Hellreaver attacked the pizzas Vlad had brought for them while he and Mae sat down to eat.

"How was your day?" Vlad said.

"Busy."

Mae took a moment to savor the rich bite she'd just taken. She didn't realize she'd moaned out loud until she noticed Vlad's heated stare. The incubus looked like he was considering skipping dinner and going straight for dessert. Mae's stomach fluttered. She swallowed heavily and gulped down some wine.

Her next words sobered Vlad up.

"I think the Dark Council are up to no good again."

She told him about Hodge's autopsy findings and the suspicions she'd discussed with the High Council. Vlad tensed when she mentioned Candice Reese's magic ability.

Mae studied him curiously. "What?"

"A Fire Magic user?" Vlad repeated guardedly.

"Yeah. Bryony said they're pretty rare these days."

Vlad's face had clouded over. "They are."

He resumed eating.

Mae stared. It was clear he knew something about Fire Magic.

"That's it?" she said skeptically.

Vlad grimaced. "I'll tell you more, if it becomes relevant one day."

Mae hesitated before relenting. The incubus wasn't one to play games when it came to the important stuff.

There must be a reason why he doesn't want to talk about it.

"What about your day?" She raised an eyebrow. "Shot anyone? Indulged in some extortion? Strung someone up in your bat cave and whipped them into submission?"

Vlad looked hurt. "I sat in an office and did paperwork."

Mae grinned. "The gangster life isn't as exciting as I thought it would be."

A flare of incubus energy danced across her skin. She shivered, her blood warming in response to it.

Vlad's mouth stretched in a smile that almost melted her panties.

"If you're looking for excitement, I'll be more than happy to oblige, my queen."

Mae's pulse quickened. She grabbed her wine glass and inhaled the rest of the contents. There was a noise next to the table. They looked over.

Brimstone, Hellreaver, and Tarang had finished eating and were watching them with keen interest.

Twenty bucks says he gets to second base tonight, Brimstone said.

Make that fifty, Hellreaver countered.

Tarang rumbled something. Brimstone and Hellreaver sucked in air and gave the tiger an admiring glance.

That's sick, the fox mumbled.

Vlad sighed. "If you hold that any tighter, you'll break it."

Mae unclenched her fingers from the stem of her glass and glared at the familiars and the weapon. "Next time, the three of you are eating in the corridor outside."

They bristled indignantly at that.

"By the way, I'll be headed to Prague this weekend on business," Vlad interjected hastily. "Make sure you don't get into any trouble while I'm away."

Mae blinked. "You are?" Ire replaced her surprise. Her mouth pressed into a thin line. "And what am I, five?"

Vlad's teasing smile slowly faded. "The Dark Council may be up to no good there too, although I am not certain what they could be trying to achieve."

Mae's fingers tightened on her knife and fork. "What do you mean?"

"I'll let you know if I find something," he replied evasively. "Incidentally, I haven't seen Alicia around lately."

"She's on a trip to Hell," Mae said. "Something about seeing to her troops."

Alicia Calvarro was the Queen of Soul Reapers. She'd been working with them for some time in her capacity as the demon Astarte's representative while wearing the disguise of an FBI Special Agent.

They'd just finished dessert and were clearing the table when Mae's cell chimed with an incoming video call. Her stomach flip-flopped when she saw the caller ID. It was Nikolai.

Irritation prickled her skin and dampened some of her elation. *Took him long enough!*

"How about we put that in the dishwasher?" Vlad said nastily.

He indicated her phone. Mae narrowed her eyes at the incubus and moved to the window to take the call.

Nikolai appeared on the screen. Moonlight washed across his face where he stood on a dark balcony, the only other illumination the soft glow of lamps visible through the curtains billowing behind him.

"Hey," the sorcerer said, contrite. "Sorry I haven't called until now."

Mae's disgruntlement dissipated at his weary expression. "You look like death warmed over."

"He should stay dead," Vlad muttered from across the room.

Nikolai's features tightened. "Who was that?"

Mae pursed her lips, feeling guilty even though she had no reason to. "Er, Vlad's here."

Nikolai's gaze grew frosty. "Why?"

"He made dinner."

A muscle twitched in Nikolai's jawline. "How many times has he made you dinner since I left?"

Mae scratched her cheek.

"I can't remember," she said evasively.

"Nine." Vlad came over and directed a smug smile at Nikolai over Mae's shoulder. "And tonight's the night we test her bedsprings—*ow!*"

He winced and rubbed the spot on his ribs Mae had just stabbed with an elbow.

"No one is testing anyone's bedsprings," she ground out.

"That's cold, Princess," he murmured with mock dejection.

He moved to clear the rest of the table.

Mae chewed her lip as she observed the dark circles under Nikolai's eyes. "Is training not going well?"

"It is. Alastair and I have learned a lot from the Council of the Moon."

The crow flew out of the room behind Nikolai and landed on his shoulder. He peeked at Mae and squawked a welcome.

She greeted the familiar before lowering her brows. "What's wrong, then?"

Nikolai hesitated. "Marlena said I'm trying to do too much too fast."

Mae stared, puzzled.

The slight color that stained the sorcerer's cheekbones was visible even in the gloom. He rubbed the back of his neck awkwardly.

"It's because I want to come back to New York as soon as I can."

Mae's chest swelled at the words he didn't say and the banked heat brightening his eyes. She'd never asked Nikolai if he intended to stay with his family in Prague and join the Council of the Moon, like Marlena wanted him to. She'd been too scared to find out what his answer would be.

She bit her lip to stop a goofy smile from spreading across her face.

Vlad made gagging noises behind her.

Nikolai's expression grew chilly. "When is that asshole leaving?"

CHAPTER SIX

Roman Savelich's gut tightened as he followed his best friend out a fire door at the side of their dormitory building. Someone had tampered with the alarm sensor and propped it open slightly. The gap was wide enough for Vincent Rochette to slip his fingers through, but not big enough to catch the attention of the security guard who would soon be doing his rounds.

Vincent seemed unconcerned that they were breaking all sorts of school regulations by sneaking out of their dorms in the middle of the night. If anything, his bright eyes and flushed expression denoted his excitement at tonight's illicit adventure.

From what Roman had deduced, this wasn't the first time he'd done this. Roman wasn't ignorant of the fact that many of the seniors at the international school he attended in Prague regularly sneaked out to enjoy the various pleasures the city's nightlife had to offer. As the student with the best grades in his class and the one most likely to become head of the student council next year, he didn't want to sully his immaculate school record and ruin his chances of earning that role.

He knew how proud it would make his grandfather.

But Roman also couldn't ignore the fact that Vincent was headed for trouble.

The face of the boy who'd led his best friend astray loomed out of the shadows under a row of trees as they crossed Italská Street. Flanking Zak Byrne were four others. They all belonged to wealthy families, just as Roman and Vincent did.

Zak smirked when he saw Roman. "I'm surprised you agreed to tag along, Savelich."

Roman met his gaze steadily. At five foot eight, he had a good few inches on Zak. "I wanted to see what all the fuss was about."

Zak's eyes darkened with irritation at his calm tone. A gleeful look flitted across his face before he assumed his usual nonchalant mask.

"Let's go. We don't want to be late."

Roman frowned. *What was that about?*

If Vincent noticed Zak's odd expression, he didn't say anything.

Roman hadn't been aware of his best friend falling under the influence of Zak and his gang until a couple of weeks ago, something he deeply regretted. Usually an open book, Vincent had become more secretive of late, a warning sign Roman would have noted had he not been preoccupied with other matters. By the time he'd realized what was happening, the Canadian teenager was already involved with the unsavory crowd.

Roman was conscious of the rumors circulating about Zak and his cronies. They were thought to be responsible for the trade of street drugs that had plagued the school recently. But the teachers didn't have any concrete evidence to support their suspicions. Add to that the boys' families exerting pressure on the headmaster not to stir trouble, and the whole affair had pretty much been swept under the carpet.

But it wasn't just concern for Vincent that had Roman accepting their invitation to go with them tonight. Their latest hobby had piqued his interest. According to Vincent, Zak and his friends had made contact with somebody involved in the occult.

They cut through Riegrovy Park and emerged opposite Prague City University. Roman noted how Zak avoided the main streets and kept to narrow roads as they made their way south. His brow wrinkled.

It was clear Zak and his friends had taken this route plenty of times before. Roman wondered if it was because it lessened the risk of them being spotted by someone they knew. Some of the teachers at their international school lived in Prague's second district after all.

Even though Roman couldn't see them, he knew the bodyguards his grandfather had assigned to him wouldn't be far behind. Having an escort was something he hadn't been overly enthused about when he'd first started attending the school and he'd fought tooth and nail not to have them. But he hadn't been able to argue with his grandfather after the latter had explained the stark reasons for the guards.

As the top executive of an influential humanitarian organization, Budimir Volkov had received many a death threat throughout the years. It seemed some of his enemies had become aware of Roman's existence and harbored nefarious intentions toward him, despite Roman assuming the name Savelich to hide his identity.

The gothic spires of the Church of St. Ludmila rose against the dark sky to the west when they crossed Korunni Street, the stone facade of the 19th century basilica shining brightly under the spotlights in Peace Square. The bells tolled the midnight hour as they strolled past a tram stop.

Goosebumps broke out across Roman's flesh as he listened to the chimes. He couldn't help but sense an ominous undertone to them. He chided himself the next instant.

It wasn't like him to be superstitious.

A group of inebriated men emerged from a liquor store and stumbled into their path as they entered a small square. They veered around them and carried on south for some thousand feet before turning east.

Roman masked a grimace when he realized their destination.

I guess it kinda makes sense. That place is perfect if you want to smoke pot and play pretend magic.

The pale, stone columns flanking the ancient gatehouse of Grébovka Park appeared at the end of the road. Zak ignored the locked entrance and turned left into a cobbled, residential street lined with pastel-colored, Neo-Baroque apartment buildings. He stopped, looked around furtively, and rapidly scaled the iron fence separating them from the park. His friends followed as he dropped down soundlessly between two irregular rock formations.

Roman slowed.

"Come on," Vincent urged in a low voice as he headed after them.

Unease knotted Roman's shoulders as he glanced over his shoulder. He couldn't see his escort.

They can't be far behind.

He checked that the GPS tracker on his cell phone was switched on and eyed the bright windows beyond the balconies of the apartments overlooking the street. No one seemed to be looking his way.

Vincent hissed his name.

Roman wiped his suddenly sweaty palms on his jeans. He hesitated, steeled himself, and climbed the railing. Sneaking out of school was one thing. Breaking and entering a public space owned by the city was another.

Zak and his friends were already past a triumphal, stone archway and on the upper terrace of the Grotta, the artificial cave system the park was famous for. Arranged over three levels, the complex of shallow grottos and niches overlooked a fountain holding a statue of the god Neptune.

The harsh light of Vincent's cell phone painted ghoulish shadows across his features and the mysterious spaces they passed as he led the way down the narrow, convoluted steps flowing down the slope. They reached the second-floor terrace moments behind Zak and his cronies.

Zak stood with his face cast in shadows in a doorway to the left. "Over here."

Roman startled a little at his stiff tone. He sounded on edge for the first time that evening. A faint frown marred Vincent's brow.

They followed Zak and his gang down a spiral staircase to a semi-circular arcade on the first floor of the Grotta. Roman's skin prickled when they stepped out from under the promenade and onto the mosaic terrace overlooking the fountain. The statue of Neptune loomed in the center of the water feature ahead of them.

The dark god looked like he was condemning them to a dark fate as he bore witness to their felonious presence.

Roman tensed when he caught movement to his right.

A man emerged from the gloom of a vine-covered archway.

Zak jumped, startled. He pressed a hand to his chest and laughed nervously. "Jesus! You almost gave me a heart attack."

The stranger ignored him and scanned their group. His gaze landed on Vincent and Roman. "Which one is Roman?"

Zak smirked and pointed a finger. "The blond."

Vincent lowered his brows. "What's going on, Zak? Who is this guy?"

Roman's heartbeat quickened. He could tell his best friend was unaware of whatever arrangement Zak appeared to have made with the stranger. He also knew that they were in trouble.

The man was a magic user. He was certain of it.

But that wasn't what had alarmed him. He could sense something coming from the guy. Something he'd never felt before and which made his stomach churn.

A gray cat padded out of one of the grottos and leapt onto the sorcerer's shoulder. Roman swallowed. From the others' lack of reaction, he was certain the creature was a familiar and that no one else could see it.

"You got the goods?" Zak challenged. "A deal's a deal, Devin."

The sorcerer's mouth stretched in a smile that didn't reach his eyes. "Of course. Here, catch."

He extracted something from his coat and tossed it at Zak. It was a clear bag filled with thin cannabis rolls.

Zak almost dropped it in his haste to open it. He pulled out one of the homemade sticks, brought it to his nose, and inhaled deeply. Pleasure brightened his face.

"Sweet." He handed Devin a roll of bills and flashed a mocking smile at Roman. "So, what do you want with our friend here? Is it something to do with this Fire Magic Vincent told us about?"

Zak's friends sniggered as he shared the cannabis cigarettes with them.

Vincent paled. "What?!"

He cast a guilty look at Roman.

Roman fisted his hands and silently cursed his best friend. He'd inadvertently told Vincent his secret a year ago, in a moment of weakness. Truth be told, he hadn't thought Vincent had believed him. After all, he'd never shown him his powers.

Did he tell them because he wanted to impress them?!

"Look, I—I was joking when I said that!" Vincent stammered, his gaze swinging wildly between Zak and Devin. "Besides, we all know that stuff's not real!"

A voice coiled out of the darkness. "That's where you're wrong."

CHAPTER SEVEN

ROMAN WHIRLED AROUND. A MAN WITH RED HAIR AND A reptilian gaze was climbing the shallow steps to the terrace, a tawny lynx coiling around his legs.

Every instinct Roman possessed told him to run.

Zak frowned at the stranger and took his cigarette out of his mouth. "Who are you?" He glanced at Devin, suspicion clouding his face. His tone turned accusing. "You told me it would just be you tonight."

The red-haired man smiled.

Fear rooted Roman's legs to the ground.

Vincent must have caught on to the sinister mood pervading the terrace. He clutched Roman's arm and pulled him back a step, his face pasty with apprehension.

"Quite the little mercenary you've found there, Devin," the red-haired man drawled.

Devin bobbed his head respectfully. "He will be dealt with presently, Master."

A choking noise broke the tense lull even as Roman

considered the ominous meaning behind the sorcerer's deferential address. His head whipped around. Acid burned the back of his throat.

"Oh God!" Vincent mumbled.

One of Zak's friends was slowly turning purple. The vessels in his sclera ruptured, rendering his eyes grotesquely red. He dropped his cannabis roll and clutched his throat on a panicked wheeze.

The other three gaped. Red blotches filled the whites of their eyes the next instant. They started coughing and wheezing.

All four fell to the ground, fingers clawing at their windpipes as they struggled to breathe.

Alarm rounded Zak's eyes. "What the—?!" He glared at Devin. "What did you do to my friends, asshole?!"

"The same thing I did to you," Devin replied coldly.

Zak's gaze dropped to the cannabis stick in his hand. He cast it to the ground as if it were a snake. Terror leeched the color from his face as his friends started to convulse and foam at the mouth, backs arching and legs kicking out in violent spasms.

"No, no, no!" he mumbled.

Zak yanked his cell out of his pocket and began dialing a number. He cried out as the device was ripped from his hand by an invisible force that crushed two of his fingers. Hemorrhages bloomed on his sclera even as he blanched in pain. His lips turned blue.

An incoherent sound left Vincent as he stared at Zak's cell where it floated in mid-air. His hand dug painfully into Roman's arm.

Zak fell to the ground and started thrashing around.

Roman's heart slammed a panicked tempo against his ribs.

Something moved on his right shoulder. It shifted closer, invisible to all but him as its scaly flesh cooled his hot cheek.

The man with the red hair crushed Zak's cell phone with a bored flick of a finger before starting toward them. They backed away.

"Vincent?" Roman murmured through numb lips as he watched the sorcerer approach.

"Yeah?" his best friend mumbled.

"Get ready to run!"

Roman saw Vincent cast a wild glance at him out the corner of his eye. He kept his attention focused on the red-haired man. He knew instinctively that to look away was to invite instant death.

"My bodyguards will be here soon," he said in a voice that sounded shockingly steady even to his own ears. "It will be in your interest if you leave. Right *now.*"

The red-haired sorcerer slowed to a stop and cocked his head to the side. "Your bodyguards won't be coming to rescue you anytime soon, kid." He smirked. "They're dead."

Roman's legs grew weak. He knew the sorcerer wasn't lying.

Vincent whimpered beside him.

"Now, how about you show us some of that Fire Magic?" the red-haired sorcerer drawled.

His lynx hissed, her eyes darkening to a vile obsidian.

Roman's ears popped as the pressure around them dropped. The air became heavy with an insidious power. Vincent choked on his next breath.

Heat filled Roman's belly as he called upon the magic within his core. It became fractionally easier to breathe again.

He inhaled and invoked a spell a heartbeat before the sorcerer's attack could crush them. *"Fire Shield!"*

A wall of flames burst into life a foot from his outstretched right hand, the center of the conflagration quickly merging to form complex, defensive runes. Power bubbled through his veins and that of his familiar as she finally emerged from invisibility where she gripped his shoulder with her claws.

The barrier vibrated violently when the red-haired sorcerer's magic smashed into it. The man smiled with savage satisfaction.

"A veiled chameleon." He studied Roman's familiar with a sneer. "Clever." He met Roman's furious gaze. "Looks like you won't bore me after all, kid."

Filomena hissed, her tongue darting out to taste the air and her casque quivering. Roman could sense her fear.

"Run!" he barked at Vincent.

Frustration churned his gut when his best friend remained rooted to the ground, his horrified gaze locked on the shield of fire.

Roman raised his left hand and cast a magic blast.

The shockwave lifted Vincent off his feet and

carried him past Neptune's statue and beyond the fountain. A startled cry left him when he landed on the ground with a bone-jarring thud.

"*Go, goddammit!*" Roman yelled.

Tears glittered on Vincent's face as he gazed at him, distraught. He scrambled to his hands and knees, rose, and stumbled into the gloom.

Devin moved to intercept him.

"Let him go," the red-haired man said dismissively. "He is of no consequence."

Devin stopped and dipped his head. "As you wish, Master."

Vincent vanished between the trees.

Roman's relief was short-lived. The look the red-haired sorcerer was giving him sent ice skittering down his spine. He felt like an insect under a magnifying glass. One that was about to be dissected alive.

"Filomena," he mumbled.

The chameleon made a low, grinding noise at his warning. She pressed her body against his cheek, her scales growing warm. Her power poured through their bond and amplified his magic.

Roman didn't know what these two men wanted with him. But one thing he was certain of. If they captured him, it would be the last he would see of this world for some time, if not ever.

His gaze swung from the red-haired sorcerer to Devin. There was a slim chance he could take the guy down. But he was no match for his master.

That didn't mean he would go down without a fight though.

Regret twisted Roman's heart. He swallowed.

I'm sorry, Grandfather.

Budimir Volkov had sent him to Prague to protect him from the Vissarions after his mother Alina passed away. As the one and only heir to have manifested the Vissarion bloodline's potent Fire Magic after Katarina Vissarion's death over two decades ago, he was a rare specimen the noble family of sorcerers and witches would seek to confine and mold to their will so as to reclaim the esteem they once commanded in the world of magic.

Roman had promised his grandfather he would never practice his sorcery and would lay low so as not to garner the attention of any magic user whose path he might inadvertently cross.

He'd lied.

"*Disperse,*" the red-haired sorcerer said dispassionately.

The fire shield wavered and started to dissipate.

Roman clenched his jaw and drew on his core. "*Ignite!*"

The air thinned as a blaze exploded into existence across the terrace, consuming all the oxygen in the atmosphere. Devin cursed and raised a shield when the flames washed over him. He patted briskly at his burning clothes, his magic barrier barely holding the fire back.

"Impressive."

Roman's gaze found the red-haired sorcerer as he

and his lynx stepped out of the conflagration, bodies unscathed. His heart thundered in his chest when he saw the translucent shield of darkness enveloping them.

Shit. He clenched his jaw. *Looks like I have no choice but to try that!*

Filomena squeaked worriedly when she sensed his intent.

Roman raised a fire shield around himself, lifted the chameleon off his shoulder, and dropped to one knee. He slammed his palm down onto the ground and focused, the heat of the runes dancing gently across his skin as they sizzled and hissed.

Come on! Where are you?!

The red-haired sorcerer had stiffened outside the bubble protecting him. "What are you—?"

Roman's chest swelled with elation when he found what he was looking for. It was a thin thread of magic running deep underground. He followed the path of the ley line to its nexus, grasped the heart of unimaginable power pulsing at its center, and guided it into his body.

He gasped as a white blaze suffused his blood and his very bones, a river of blinding light that robbed him of breath and sight. Roman ground his teeth, gathered the spell he wished to invoke, and let it loose.

"*FROSTFIRE!*"

Magic detonated across the terrace, filling it with incandescent flames of ice. Devin grunted when an ivory lance pierced his thigh. The red-haired sorcerer swore and raised a second shield around himself and the lynx.

Roman blinked sweat out of his eyes as the spell started to take its toll on his body. He caught the man's hateful glare and bared his teeth in a mocking smile.

The red-haired sorcerer's brow furrowed.

"*Rot!*" he snarled.

Pressure slammed into Roman. He grunted as he hit the ground hard. Black dots bloomed across his vision when he cracked his chin on the tile.

Filomena hissed in his grasp.

The shield of fire protecting them trembled. Pain gripped Roman as the red-haired sorcerer's magic washed over him, so sudden and fierce it brought tears to his eyes. He screamed in agony as every muscle in his body locked in violent spasms. His consciousness flickered. Filomena shuddered.

Frostfire quivered and started to fade.

No! I—I can't let them get their hands on both of us!

Desperation lit Roman's veins with a final surge of adrenaline. Filomena struggled in his grip, her terror and sorrow piercing his heart and soul as she grasped his design. Roman knew he had but seconds left to act. He took a shuddering breath and mumbled a spell he'd only just learned.

"*Trans...migrate...*"

The flow of magic pouring through his core reversed itself.

Frostfire shrank and vanished with a whoosh inside his hand, where he held Filomena. It followed a path to the ley line and the nexus of power beneath the city, dragging his familiar with it.

"No!" The red-haired sorcerer swore as the chameleon's body started to fade. *"Disperse!"*

The fire shield shattered a heartbeat after Filomena vanished.

Roman finally found a word for the vile magic pressing heavily into his flesh. Corruption. His throat tightened as his grandfather's face rose before him.

I'm sorry, Grandpa! I wish...I wish I'd had time to say... my goodbyes...

Darkness clouded the edges of his vision as awareness slipped away. He blinked when a strange pulse echoed through his core.

The world went black before he could make sense of it.

CHAPTER EIGHT

Mae yawned loudly as she poured herself a coffee.

One would think you didn't get a wink of sleep last night, my witch, Brimstone observed.

Hellreaver thrummed against her breastbone. *Were your dreams filled with acts of debauchery involving you and the incubus?*

Mae gripped the medallion hard and let loose a flare of crimson magic.

"What was that?" she said menacingly.

I take it back! I take it back! the weapon protested in a strangled voice.

Mae sniffed and let go. She wasn't going to tell them that her dreams had indeed been filled with lewd fantasies involving the incubus *and* a certain white-magic sorcerer. She swallowed a sigh.

I'm gonna shrivel up like a dried prune if my nether areas don't see some action soon.

Brimstone caught her glum thought and cast a scathing look at her before addressing Hellreaver.

You're an idiot. You know how grumpy she is when she hasn't eaten.

Hellreaver pouted and grew heavy around her neck.

Brimstone's nose twitched. *Mae?*

"Yeah?"

Your eggs are burning.

"Shit!"

She was chowing down the last of her overdone breakfast when her cell rang with an incoming call. It was Raven.

"How come you guys are all video calling these days?" Mae asked thinly when the witch appeared on the screen.

Raven arched an eyebrow. "Can't a witch see her pretty queen's face?"

Mae curled her lip at the obvious sarcasm lacing Raven's words. "At this rate, I'm gonna age from overexposure."

Raven grinned. "We like to see the funny faces Brimstone makes behind you. He has his *'I can't believe she just said something so stupid'* eye roll down to a T."

Mae scowled at the fox.

What? he said defensively. *It's true. You should hear some of the stuff that comes out of your mouth.*

Mae grumbled something rude under her breath.

"Why are you calling?" she asked the witch.

Raven's expression sobered. "It's about what you told me to look into."

Mae tensed.

"There was another witch and a sorcerer in the country who officially registered Fire Magic as one of their abilities besides Candice Reese," Raven said. "I found three more who probably have Fire Magic too."

"Where are they?"

A muscle jumped in Raven's cheek. "The first two are dead. The other three are missing."

Mae's stomach dropped. "Dead?"

Brimstone padded closer.

"Yeah," Raven said grimly. "The ones who went missing were in San Francisco, Milwaukee, and Albuquerque. All three vanished in the last month, under vastly differing circumstances. Their covens are still looking for them."

A dark foreboding spread through Mae at the witch's words. "And the dead ones?"

Raven's face tightened. "A brother and sister in Salem."

Mae straightened in her seat. *That's not far from here!*

"Salem P.D. is treating their deaths as homicides and is actively investigating with the help of Boston P.D.," Raven explained.

"When did they die?"

"Ten days ago. Their funerals are taking place this afternoon."

Mae's fingers clenched on her cell. "I take it autopsies were performed?"

Raven nodded. "Yes, before the bodies were released to the family. The Boston coven and its local chapter has taken over the burial arrangements."

Mae opened her mouth.

Raven put up a hand and stopped her. "I've already made arrangements with their family for you to examine the bodies. Your ride should be with you any minute now."

Relief surged through Mae. "Thanks." She paused. "Any news on Candice Reese's familiar?"

Raven's face darkened. "You were right. Charred animal bones were discovered not far from her body. They were likely the remains of her familiar."

Her Asian vine snake hissed softly on her shoulder. The witch petted the creature gently.

Mae frowned heavily as she ended the call. She phoned Jared, told him what she needed, and brought up Hodge's number next.

"Steve, I've had an emergency come up. I'm gonna have to take the day off."

A short pause followed.

"Does this have anything to do with what I showed you last night?"

Her boss sounded resigned, as if he'd been expecting her call.

"Yeah." Guilt twisted Mae's belly. "I may have to go MIA for more than a day. Are you going to be able to cope without me?"

"We'll cope. Just…be careful."

She sensed a pair of magic users approaching her place just as she was lacing up her boots. Recognition washed over her. Mae rose and opened her door just as Miles Nolan raised his hand to knock.

"Surprise," Violet drawled beside him. "Raven asked us to babysit you for the day."

"She said not to let you drive," Miles explained pointedly.

Mae rolled her eyes, grabbed her keys, and locked up. She brought the cousins up to speed as they headed for the interstate that would take them north through Queens and Flushing.

Violet tapped her fingers on the steering wheel of the SUV.

"Fire Magic?" she said skeptically.

"Yeah," Mae said. "From what Bryony said, it's pretty rare these days."

"Is it like Sun Magic?" Miles asked curiously.

Mae shook her head. "Not from what Bryony told me last night." She chewed her lip. "I think someone used black magic infused with a demon's power on Candice Reese's core and it imploded and killed her and her familiar."

A frown marred Violet's brow. "And you suspect the Dark Council is involved?"

"I can't think of anyone else who'd be able to combine the two." Mae shrugged. "They've got Farago after all."

Miles grimaced. "True. And we saw what that dirtbag was capable of in Philadelphia." The sorcerer's expression grew puzzled. "But why are they killing Fire Magic users?"

"I don't know." Mae hesitated. "But something tells me their intention wasn't to kill them."

Understanding brightened Violet's face. "You think it's another experiment by the Dark Council?"

"Yeah," Mae replied glumly.

It was lunchtime when they reached the funeral home in Salem where the bodies were being kept for viewing ahead of the burial ceremony. It was a pretty, white-clapboard Georgian building with a recessed porch flanked by columns and rhododendron bushes. Mae, Violet, and Miles offered their condolences to the family before heading to the back room where the open caskets had been temporarily moved.

Mae's stomach twisted when she entered the preparation chamber and beheld Philip and Robin Glass. They were around her age and looked serene in death. Born two years apart, they'd been members of the Boston coven and the Salem chapter for just under eighteen months.

She clenched her jaw until it ached.

They wouldn't have stood a chance against the Dark Council.

The Salem witch overseeing their visit looked on nervously as Mae stepped up to the coffins. She'd already asked the funeral director and the mortician to step out of the room.

"What exactly are you looking for?" the woman asked hesitantly.

She shot a wary glance at Brimstone.

"Signs that they were killed with black magic," Mae replied distractedly.

The Salem witch blanched.

Mae ignored her. She'd already picked up on a faint trace of the sinister energy she'd detected when she'd examined Candice Reese's missing core.

You feel that?

Brimstone propped his forelegs on the edge of

Philip Glass's coffin. A low growl rumbled from his chest as he took a careful inhale. *Yes.*

Mae found the circular burn mark Candice Reese's corpse had exhibited on both Glass siblings.

"That's where the spell that killed them entered their bodies?" Violet asked quietly as she observed the blemish on Philip Glass's abdomen.

"I think so."

Mae had seen the reports of the autopsies that had been carried out on the siblings, courtesy of Jared accessing them through his connections in the Immortal societies. The scorch areas on the surface of their intestines and their missing blood had been written up as unexplained findings.

She knew the cops would never find the culprits behind the murders.

Mae fisted her hands and searched the worktops in the room with her gaze. She spotted what she was looking for, slipped on a pair of examination gloves, and carried the items over to Robin Glass's coffin.

The Salem witch startled. "What are you doing with those?"

"I'm going to examine her artery."

"I—I can't let you do that!" the woman protested.

"It'll be all right," Miles reassured the shocked witch. "She knows what she's doing."

Mae exposed Robin Glass's neck, placed a kidney dish against her cold skin, and made a short incision over her left carotid. She clamped off a section of the vessel and carefully drained the embalming fluid within it before spreading the stiff walls open.

The hairs rose on her nape when she spied the same weird lesions she'd spotted in Candice Reese's carotid and femoral arteries.

Violet peered over her shoulder. "What are those?"

Miles narrowed his eyes. "Aren't they…blisters?"

Mae's pulse quickened at the sorcerer's words. "You're right! I couldn't figure out what they were."

Her mind raced as she tried to put together the pieces of the puzzle.

Fire Magic and an imploded core. So, the blisters can only mean—

Bile burned the back of Mae's throat when realization finally dawned.

"The lack of lividity makes sense now," she mumbled numbly.

Violet and Miles stared at her, confused.

In what way? Brimstone said guardedly.

Mae's heart slammed violently against her ribs. "I think their blood boiled and evaporated inside their bodies."

CHAPTER NINE

The alarm woke Nikolai up at 6:30 a.m. He rolled over groggily, managed to grab his cell on the third try, and turned off the sound. Feathers fluttered warmly against his cheek.

Nikolai opened his eyes and looked blearily at Alastair where the crow rested on the pillow next to him.

"How come you look as fresh as a daisy and I feel like shit?" he mumbled accusingly.

Alastair squawked softly and nudged him with his beak.

Nikolai sighed, lifted the covers, and climbed out of bed.

He had no one to blame but himself for his fatigue. He'd been working himself even harder to master the skills he'd learned since he'd come to Prague ever since he'd spoken to Mae two nights ago.

Truth be told, he missed New York, far more than

he ever thought he would. A grimace twisted his mouth as he headed into the bathroom.

Who are you kidding? The one you really miss is her.

Nikolai's belly clenched at the emotions swirling inside him.

He'd gone to New York to awaken Mae and to request that she allow him to fight by her side against the Dark Council, so as to stop his father's mad plans and avenge his mother's death.

He hadn't expected to fall in love with the woman destined to rule the world of magic.

The realization that he'd lost his heart to the Witch Queen had come to him not as an epiphany but a slow, growing conviction, like a river molded the pebbles and rocks beneath it, or waves carved an indelible pattern into a coastline.

Living with Mae these past two months had been sweet torture. On the one hand, her apartment felt more like a home to him than anywhere he'd ever lived before. On the other, not being able to tell her how he felt. To kiss her. To touch her. All of it was slowly robbing him of his sanity.

It didn't help that a predatory incubus who oozed sex appeal was circling her like a vulture.

Nikolai frowned. *I should neuter that guy.*

He showered, dressed, and left his room to go find breakfast.

His dark thoughts abated as he navigated the corridors of the dormitory of the Council of the Moon, his footsteps echoing quietly on the tiled floor and against imposing, stone walls. He'd shocked Marlena and the other members of her council when he'd insisted on staying at the headquarters instead of the sumptuous Stanisic family mansion in a northwest suburb of the city.

Truth be told, he wasn't used to luxury. Though his rooms in the Dark Council's headquarters in Budapest weren't exactly a pauper's place, the stark decor adopted by the Sorcerer King and his acolytes in all their domains had always been oppressive rather than welcoming. His father had also never been one to shower opulence on either of his heirs.

There were two reasons why Nikolai had insisted on residing in the dormitory. Though the Stanisics had been more than effusive in welcoming him back into the fold, he couldn't stop the little voice of doubt at the back of his mind telling him not to trust them. The one that insisted they only wanted to use him for their own goals, especially now that he'd demonstrated his ability to tap into ley lines.

Nikolai clenched his jaw.

He felt like a cad for even questioning Marlena's affection and that of Klara and his extended family. Deep down inside, he knew they were being sincere. But he couldn't help himself from keeping his guard up in their presence. From the sad look he sometimes saw Marlena give him, he suspected she was aware of the internal battle being waged inside him. His face tightened.

The Dark Council and my father really did a number on me, huh?

The other reason he'd wanted to stay at the

headquarters was because of the private library of the Council of the Moon. He'd spent almost every morning there since he'd first come to Prague, poring over the rare texts few had ever had the privilege to access.

I should ask Marlena if she'll let Mae read them too.

It dawned on Nikolai that the Witch Queen likely had no use for books on magic. After all, she was Azazel's daughter, the fallen angel who had taught magic to humankind. His power was engraved in her DNA.

The tantalizing smell of cooked food distracted Nikolai from his musings as he approached the dining room.

It was empty, bar a small group seated at a table. Only half the rooms in the dormitory were ever occupied at any one time and those mainly by the apprentice sorcerers and witches in residence. Not many were up at this hour.

The handful of novices he passed murmured a greeting, their eyes full of respect. Nikolai dipped his head awkwardly in response.

It had been a couple of weeks since Marlena had asked his permission to allow both new recruits and the more established sorcerers and witches of the Council of the Moon to observe their afternoon training sessions. Nikolai hadn't minded. What he hadn't taken into account was that demonstrating his ability to access ley lines would make him a star overnight, a status he'd never get used to.

I wonder if this is what Mae feels like when people call her Queen.

"You're up early again," the cook said somewhat accusingly as he dished out a healthy portion of fried breakfast onto Nikolai's tray.

Alastair made an approving noise when the man placed a bowl of fruits and seeds next to Nikolai's plate.

Nikolai smiled faintly. "No rest for the wicked."

The cook narrowed his eyes before stabbing a spatula at him. "You really should stop talking as if you're the son of Satan."

Nikolai made a face. "I kinda am."

The cook, a retired sorcerer, shook his head. So did the newt perched on his hat.

"You keep forgetting who gave birth to you, kid," he grumbled. "Your mother was no bride of Satan."

An unexpected wave of grief constricted Nikolai's throat at his words. Gabriela Stanisic had indeed been the very opposite of all that was evil in his life.

He swallowed. "You're right."

The cook's face softened at his expression. "Now, go chow down. I get the feeling Julius won't let you off easy today."

Nikolai made a face. Julius Vlach was Marlena's second-in-command and the most powerful Moon Magic sorcerer on the continent. To say that he'd kicked Nikolai's ass on a regular basis during the first two weeks of his training would be an understatement.

He ate hastily and spent most of the morning in the library before availing himself of the private chamber Marlena had reserved for him in the basement to practice his magic. It was late afternoon by the time he emerged and made his way to the council's main training ground.

Built like an ancient Roman amphitheater, it occupied an immense, central courtyard in the headquarters. An orb that mimicked the moon levitated high above the arena, protecting the area with a barrier at the same time as it enhanced the inherent power of the sorcerers and witches born with Moon Magic.

Julius was chatting with Marlena and Klara near the entrance to the arena.

His face brightened when he saw Nikolai. "Niko!"

He came over and greeted Nikolai with a hearty slap on the back strong enough to break his bones. His hawk squawked a welcome to Alastair.

Nikolai winced. "I told you I hated that nickname."

Julius's eyes glinted with a hint of steel. "And I told you I'd stop calling you Niko the day you beat me hands down with Moon Magic, kid."

Nikolai lowered his brows. "You're only ten years older than me."

CHAPTER TEN

Marlena and Klara approached, their familiars at their sides.

"Good morning," Nikolai's aunt said with a gentle smile.

Her black terrier woofed a hello.

"Did you sleep well?" Klara asked anxiously.

Her ferret's nose twitched amicably where he was wrapped around her shoulders.

Nikolai's face relaxed in a wry grin. "If you're asking if I've rested enough for you to collectively beat me up, the answer is yes."

Marlena had the grace to look abashed. Klara flushed.

Truth be told, Julius had not been the only one to regularly thrash him during his training sessions. Marlena and Klara were extremely powerful Moon Magic witches in their own right.

"A little bird told me Linus is visiting next week,"

Nikolai told Klara as they made for the center of the arena.

Linus Jarrett was the sorcerer who'd represented Isabelle West at the covenstead in Philadelphia. Blackmailed into working for the Dark Council to save his High Priestess's life, he'd balked when they'd asked him to kill Klara and had valiantly risked his life to protect her instead.

Klara's expression grew flustered.

"Yes," she mumbled, her cheeks reddening.

Julius elbowed her in the side. "Oooh! So, we finally get to meet your boyfriend, huh?"

Klara looked like she wanted to sink into the ground.

Marlena sighed. "Bryony tattled?"

"It was Abraham, actually," Nikolai replied.

Even though it was late in the day, the galleries were starting to fill up with witches and sorcerers. It wasn't every day they got to witness the skills of their own leaders and the white magic of a ley-line user.

Alastair braced on Nikolai's shoulder as he assumed a defensive stance in the middle of a wide circle formed by Marlena, Klara, Julius, and their familiars.

"You ready, Niko?" Julius called out.

Nikolai reached for the banked source of power in his belly. "I was ready yesterday, *old man*."

Klara snorted. Marlena swallowed a sigh.

"Good." Julius's expression grew fierce. "*Moon Spear!*"

Nikolai raised his left hand. "*Shield!*" A pale, circular guard exploded in front of him as a bolt of dazzling light arrowed toward his chest from Julius's fingertips. He twisted on his heels and lifted his right hand as the spear smashed into his shield. "*Shield! Multiply!*"

Another two guards formed around him, blocking Marlena and Klara's near silent spells.

Sweat beaded his forehead as he and Alastair defended themselves against a relentless onslaught over the minutes that followed, the orb above the arena flickering faintly as it augmented the powers of his attackers.

"Focus on your Moon Magic, Nikolai!" Marlena snapped as one of Klara's blasts glanced off his left thigh. "Stop trying to use your white magic to defend!"

Nikolai gritted his teeth, his heart slamming against his ribs. It hadn't been until his first training session in Prague that he'd learned of his ability to use Moon Magic too. Marlena had detected a trace of it when he'd fought Barquiel in Philadelphia. She hadn't told him at the time as she wasn't sure if it had been wishful thinking on her part.

Though his mother had ultimately been known for being a powerful white-magic witch, she had also harbored Moon Magic in her core by virtue of her lineage. It seemed she had passed on her power to him.

Identifying and separating the two types of magic fused in his core had almost broken Nikolai and pushed Alastair to his very limits as a familiar those first couple of weeks. Though the process had been agonizingly slow, they were now in a position to wield Moon Magic and white magic individually.

It was only after they'd managed to do this that

Marlena and Julius had revealed how he could protect himself and Alastair from the debilitating side effects they suffered when they accessed a ley line.

Nikolai fought back his age-old instinct to reach for the white magic bubbling in his core and continued shielding himself and Alastair with his newfound power, the thin thread connecting his core to the artificial moon above the arena throbbing brightly within him. It was another ten minutes before he finally spotted an opportunity to counter the barrage of attacks hammering at his defenses.

Now!

Alastair's feathers fluttered against his cheek as he spread his wings open. The crow's eyes flared a dazzling white, his magic fusing fully with Nikolai's.

Nikolai barked out the spell they'd learned a few days ago. *"Moon Storm!"*

A tempest of pale light erupted around them. Alastair's claws sank into his shoulder as it boomed across the arena, so loud his eardrums throbbed and his teeth rattled. Marlena, Julius, and Klara gasped when the shockwave drove them back several feet, surprise widening their eyes. The artificial moon trembled, the shield protecting the spectators in the galleries holding true.

Nikolai's chest lightened. That was the most powerful Moon Magic spell he'd cast yet.

It's not over!

He grounded his legs, aimed his hands palm down at a spot midway between his braced feet, and sent a blast of white magic into the ground. It snaked through the concrete and the very foundations of the training ground before arrowing down into the earth, as fast as lightning.

A triumphant smile stretched Nikolai's mouth when he found the potent nexus of power that lay deep beneath the headquarters of the Council of the Moon.

Something eerie brushed against his magic as he tapped into it.

What the—?!

Alastair's screeched warning reached Nikolai a second before the simmering flames that had been hidden within the nexus arrowed straight up into their bodies within a single beat of their hearts.

It was as if the fire had been waiting to consume them.

Nikolai opened his mouth on a silent scream as his and Alastair's cores went supernova. The inferno spread through his veins and bones before manifesting through his flesh, robbing him of breath even as it burned the oxygen in the air. A crimson blaze exploded around Alastair, his feathers catching fire.

The crow fell limply off his shoulder just as he hit the ground on all fours.

A cacophony of alarmed shouts sounded dimly in Nikolai's ears as he fisted his hands on the warm stone beneath him. He shook his head dazedly, fighting to remain conscious. Bright sparks drew his eyes.

The flames crackling around his fingers had turned a rich, velvet red laced with inky strands. His pulse spiked.

Though he and Alastair were on fire, their flesh remained unblemished.

How—how is that possible?!

Nikolai blinked. The pain he was experiencing wasn't from the flames eating away at his body, but the strange, new power coursing through his bloodstream. A power that had manifested outward in a crimson inferno.

A distant yell reached him. His neck muscles creaked as he turned his head a fraction. Marlena, Klara, and Julius were trying to get to him and Alastair through the conflagration filling the arena.

"Stay…back," he mumbled.

His eyes rounded.

Dozens of Moon Magic shields shone palely in the galleries of the training ground. They'd been erected by the experienced sorcerers and witches in the crowd when the barrier meant to protect the spectators had failed. Shards glinted behind Marlena and Klara where the artificial moon now lay in tatters.

Did we do that?!

Dread twisted Nikolai's stomach when his gaze found Alastair.

The crow was barely breathing.

I—I have to cut our connection to the nexus!

He shuddered as the storm raging within him threatened to consume him whole. He didn't know what this was, except that it *was* magic of some sort. And it was clashing with his Moon Magic and his white magic, like oil trying desperately to mix with water.

Mae's face rose before him. Determination filled Nikolai.

He clenched his jaw, gathered what he could of his and Alastair's powers, and yanked at the link tethering them to the nexus.

Something pulled back.

Nikolai scowled. *The hell?!*

He dug his nails into his palms and reached for the connection once more, this time aiming right at the heart of the nexus. The tendons in his neck corded as he strained against the tether.

A sinister feeling flitted through him. He could sense something within the nexus. Something that filled his veins with ice.

A roar left his throat when the connection finally tore.

The firestorm filling the center of the arena abated, the flames fizzling out as rapidly as they had formed. Sweat dripped off Nikolai's face and splashed onto the stone beneath him as he trembled and panted in the aftermath of the vanishing blaze.

Marlena reached him and dropped by his side. "Nikolai!"

Julius and Klara weren't far behind.

Julius shook Nikolai's shoulder violently. "You okay, kid?!"

"I will be if you stop doing that," Nikolai groaned.

"Oh."

Julius let go. Nikolai searched frantically for Alastair. His racing heart stuttered.

The crow was awake and looked like he'd recovered

from what had just happened to them. He was standing guard over a burning chameleon, his own feathers simmering gently still with dark red flames.

The creature's scales slowly shifted from red to a vibrant pattern of jade and sapphire as the fire engulfing it dissipated where it lay atop a jagged crack in the floor.

Nikolai's eyes widened when he saw the animal's ribcage shudder with its labored breathing.

It's alive!

Alastair clicked softly and nudged the chameleon with his head.

"What's going on?" Klara mumbled.

CHAPTER ELEVEN

Cortes arched an eyebrow. "You mean, you still don't know if I'll be able to see Volkov or not?"

I'm gonna shoot this guy.

Vlad suppressed his instincts and forced a polite smile as he settled on a leather seat opposite the *Bacatá Cartel* mobster.

"Like I said, he's proven somewhat elusive to reach since he arrived in Prague. I know where he's staying, so arranging a meeting shouldn't be a problem."

Cortes looked unconvinced by his statement. Vlad's gaze skimmed over Ilya and Milo where they were coming down the aisle of the private jet. They took up position behind and to the side of him while they studied Cortes's men with flinty eyes.

"You should tell your escort to relax." Cortes propped his neck against the headrest and closed his eyes. "It's going to be a long flight otherwise."

Vlad ignored his advice. "I thought Gomez was coming with you."

Cortes didn't reply.

Vlad made a face. "He's still alive, right?"

Cortes sighed. "I'm not a savage, Mr. Vissarion. Gomez may be a fool when it comes to certain matters, but he is loyal to a fault." He paused. "And I value loyalty above all else in this wretched life."

Vlad wasn't exactly pleased to find he had another thing in common with the Colombian. Tarang's tail flicked his legs languidly. It reminded him of the question that had occupied his mind since his last encounter with the mobster.

"How come you can see Tarang?"

Cortes opened his eyes and glanced at the tiger before fixing Vlad with a cool stare. "I didn't put you down as a talker."

Vlad's mouth stretched into a thin smile. "Humor me."

A flight attendant came over to serve them drinks. Cortes waited until the man left before answering.

"I have magic in me. I just…can't use it."

Vlad stared. "How so?"

Cortes assumed the expression of a man resigned to a fate worse than death. "Someone damaged my core and killed my familiar when I was fourteen."

Tarang lifted his head from Vlad's thigh and huffed worriedly.

Vlad gently stroked the tiger between his ears. Tarang settled back down, his slit-like eyes focused unblinkingly on Cortes.

"He can understand what I'm saying?" the Colombian asked curiously.

"To an extent. It's more like he's attuned to my emotions." Vlad studied Cortes steadily. "It sounds like you've had a challenging past."

"No more than you, I suspect. I get the feeling the stories about you growing up in a castle like some kind of fairytale prince are grossly exaggerated."

Vlad grimaced.

Cortes lifted his Scotch to his lips and observed him shrewdly while he took a leisurely sip. "Are you worried about meeting Volkov?"

Vlad refused to rise to the bait and maintained a neutral expression out of sheer habit. "Not really. What happened is in the past as far as we're concerned."

"That's very…generous of the man."

Vlad raised his glass and took a mouthful of his whiskey. A restless feeling twisted his insides as the expensive alcohol burned a smooth path down his throat.

Truth be told, he wasn't looking forward to seeing Volkov again. The last time he'd met the man in person had been at a funeral, after all.

Cortes glanced at his watch with a faint frown. He signaled to one of his guards. "Go ask the pilot what's taking so long. We should have been in the air five minutes ago."

The man nodded and made for the cockpit. It opened before he reached it. The co-pilot exited the flight deck and brushed past the bodyguard as he hurried down the aisle toward Cortes, his face pinched.

"I'm sorry, sir," he said in a rushed voice. "We have a slight situation."

Cortes observed him calmly. "What kind of situation?"

"An SUV just pulled up in our flight path."

Cortes's men reached for their guns. The co-pilot blanched. Cortes raised a hand. His men slowly lowered their hands from their weapons.

The Colombian turned his head and leveled a chilly look at Vlad. "You know anything about this, Vissarion?"

Vlad frowned and shook his head, genuinely puzzled. "I have no idea what—"

"Uh-oh," Milo mumbled.

The bodyguard was staring out of a porthole.

Tarang rose and huffed excitedly, his tail swinging ever faster.

Cortes stared at the tiger.

A sinking feeling came over Vlad. He knew the look on his familiar's face.

"What is it?" he asked Milo stiffly, praying fervently the answer wouldn't be what he was dreading it was going to be.

Ilya shattered his hopes with his next words.

"It's Mae," the bodyguard reported gruffly where he peered over Milo's shoulder. "Violet and Miles are with her."

Vlad's fingers clenched on his armrests. *Shit!*

His heartbeat picked up as he stood and crossed the aisle to a starboard porthole.

Mae's face brightened when she spotted him. She was hanging out of the passenger window of Violet's

SUV. She waved energetically, opened the door, and jumped out of the vehicle with Brimstone.

Cortes appeared next to Vlad. He furrowed his brow as he watched Mae run toward the aircraft.

"Who is this—Mae?" His frown deepened. "Is that a fox?"

"Mae Jin is the Witch Queen," Vlad replied, his face tight. "The fox is her familiar."

Cortes stared. "As in, *the* Witch Queen of prophecy?"

Vlad clenched his jaw. "Something must have happened. She wouldn't just turn up like this."

Cortes watched him for a couple of beats before asking one of his men to open the door. Mae rushed up the steps and inside the cabin, her hair fluttering wildly around her and Brimstone on her heels. Relief flooded her face when she caught sight of Vlad.

She rushed over and hugged him, oblivious to the guards staring at her and Ilya and Milo's sharp inhales. "I've been calling you all day!"

Vlad closed his arms around her, startled. He took his cell out his back pocket and cursed internally. He'd forgotten to take it off silent mode after a meeting that morning.

He grasped Mae's shoulders and pulled back slightly. "What's wrong?" He scanned her face and body, dread sending his pulse racing. "Are you hurt?!"

She shook her head. "I'm okay." Her eyes darkened. "Something's happened in Prague. We need to hitch a ride there."

"*We?*" Cortes said in a brittle tone.

Mae registered the Colombian's presence and his sour expression.

She did a slight double take. "Whoa! Someone did a right number on your magic core."

Cortes blinked, stunned. His men stiffened when Violet and Miles came inside the airplane. They were both breathless, like they'd been running.

"You sure it's safe to leave your car there?" Ilya said.

He cocked a thumb to where Violet had parked her SUV in a zone designated for emergency vehicles.

Violet waved a dismissive hand. "Someone's gonna pick it up." She dropped onto a couch and fanned herself. "I need a drink!"

"You and me both," Miles muttered as he sat beside her.

He flashed a distracted smile at one of Cortes's men.

Vlad looked into the Colombian's irate face.

"I don't think they're gonna leave," he said, contrite.

Cortes took on the appearance of a man strongly considering killing something as he observed Violet's rabbit and Miles's boa constrictor making themselves at home. He inhaled raggedly before running a hand through his hair.

"Alright," he growled. "But you owe me one."

Mae brightened. "Oh. Is this your plane?"

"Yes," Cortes said grudgingly.

He froze when Hellreaver detached himself from Mae's neck and shifted into his double-bladed, serrated dagger form. The weapon zoomed down the cabin to the galley, heedless of Cortes's men jumping out of the way with shocked gasps.

A muffled scream came from the back of the aircraft.

Mae deflated. "I'm sorry. He smelled meat."

"He only eats bad people," Ilya reassured Cortes's men where they stood clutching their guns.

Vlad sighed. "That's not exactly going to put their minds at rest considering their occupation."

"Oh." Ilya scratched his cheek. "You're right."

Brimstone's nose twitched. He licked his chops and padded toward the galley with Tarang.

"I'll bring them back," Miles said hastily at Cortes's thunderous expression. He disappeared after the familiars, Millie hissing disapprovingly where she coiled around his leg. The sorcerer's excited voice reached them a moment later. "Oh! They've got Skittles!"

Violet beamed. "Cool. Bring me a soda too, will ya?"

"I'm *really* sorry," Vlad told Cortes.

CHAPTER TWELVE

The incubus made a disgusted face. "Oh. So you were talking about Nikolai?"

Mae's mouth thinned. "Don't be like that. He's saved your ass on a few occasions now."

"He'd better be at death's door for you to be this worried about him," Vlad grumbled, stabbing his canapé with a fork and shoving it in his mouth.

A fresh bout of dread churned Mae's stomach as she recalled her conversation with Bryony that morning. The New York coven High Priestess had called to tell her there'd been an incident at the headquarters of the Council of the Moon, where Nikolai was staying. She hadn't gone into details, only to say that something had happened during his training and that Marlena wanted Mae there.

Her fear had deepened when she hadn't been able to reach Nikolai on his cell phone. It was only after Bryony had told her she would arrange a private jet to the Czech Republic later that afternoon and hung up that Mae had recalled Vlad mentioning that he would be traveling there that very day.

It hadn't taken much convincing to get Violet and Miles to take her to the airport to try and chase down Vlad's flight once she'd called his uncle's home and figured out where he was.

Mae became aware of a guarded stare and turned her head to meet Enrique Cortes's watchful gaze. From Vlad's brief introduction and the presence of an armed escort, she'd gathered he was a gangster too.

"Thanks for letting us come along."

Cortes bobbed his head, his dark gaze focused unblinkingly on her.

Mae wiped a thumb self-consciously across the corner of her mouth. "Have I got something on my face?"

She'd just inhaled three hot dogs and a can of beer.

"Forgive me," Cortes drawled. "I never thought I would live long enough to see a myth come to life."

"Oh." Mae wrinkled her nose. "You know about the prophecy, huh?"

"Every child in my coven grew up learning that story."

Vlad frowned faintly at the gangster over his glass of wine. "So, you *do* belong to a coven?"

"Belonged." Cortes waved a dismissive hand. "They kicked me out when I stopped being able to use magic. And coven is probably the wrong word. It was more like a cult."

There was a short, tense silence.

"I've never seen a cracked magic core before," Mae

said reluctantly. "Granted, I'm relatively new to this stuff myself, but I kinda get the feeling it's a miracle you survived whatever did this to you."

"It was my aunt's handiwork."

Mae's eyes widened. Vlad blinked.

Cortes smiled faintly at their shocked looks. "She felt…threatened by my abilities."

Brimstone spoke. *I can tell he would have been a powerful sorcerer. He smells of Arcane Magic.*

Mae frowned faintly at the fox. *Arcane Magic?*

It's a rare kind of magic that died out soon after Ran Soyun's passing and Azazel's banishment to Hell. It originated from the bones of the ancient gods who once walked the Earth.

Cortes's shrewd gaze swung between Mae and Brimstone, as if he could sense their silent conversation. Despite the mobster's nonchalant expression, Mae could tell he still harbored strong feelings about what had happened to him.

"So, how does one go from being a sorcerer to a gangster?"

She realized her question was brazen when she caught several of Cortes's men exchanging wary glances.

Cortes's smile thinned. "There are only three ways a boy comes out of a Medellín slum. Someone's whore. A criminal. Or a corpse."

"Ah." Mae grimaced. "Still, you should do something about your core. It may have survived the initial damage, but it's degenerating. There's a chance it will kill you somewhere down the line."

Cortes stiffened, his wine halfway to his lips. He frowned and lowered the glass. "You can tell that just by looking at me?"

"Yeah." Mae rubbed the back of her head. "It's kind of a superpower of mine."

Cortes looked like he'd just remembered something. "You're that chick from the strip club." He stared. "The one who laid into the frat boy. Gomez told me about you."

Mae's face tightened. She leaned toward Vlad.

"Wait. He's Gomez's friend?!" she hissed out the corner of her mouth.

"He's Gomez's boss and the future leader of the *Bacatá Cartel*," Vlad said drily.

Mae's stomach dropped. Violet and Miles paled.

"Relax," Cortes drawled at their expressions. "I'm hardly going to shoot the Witch Queen."

Mae laughed nervously. Cortes looked amused for once.

"By the way, did you tell your family you were leaving the country?" Vlad asked Mae curiously.

Mae's eyes bulged.

"Oh God," she mumbled numbly.

Vlad grimaced. "You didn't?"

"You forgot to tell Yoo-Mi you were going out of town?" Miles arched an eyebrow. "I am impressed."

"You are *so* dead," Violet said with a look of pity.

Ilya and Milo dipped their heads in agreement.

"Who's Yoo-Mi?" Cortes asked, nonplussed.

"Her mother," Vlad said in a commiserating tone.

Brimstone looked up from where he was sucking on a T-bone. *How about you call her now?*

"How about I call her never," Mae said glassily.

We're so screwed, Hellreaver whined.

"Wait. So, she's supposed to be some kind of crazy powerful witch, but she's scared of her mom?" one of Cortes's men murmured to Ilya.

"Her mother is a first-generation South Korean matriarch," the bodyguard said somberly.

The guy's eyes glazed over slightly. "Ah. One of those."

Cortes looked like he was trying not to laugh.

CHAPTER THIRTEEN

"Do you think you'll be able to identify this red-haired man?" Budimir Volkov asked, his tone deadly calm despite the rage bubbling in his veins.

Shivers racked Vincent Rochette's frame as he sat in the hospital bed. He glanced at Budimir's bodyguards where they framed the door of his private room before staring blindly at his lap.

"It was dark," he mumbled. "I didn't get a good look at his face." He raised his head and finally met Budimir's gaze. Though he flinched, he didn't look away. "But I—I'll try." He fisted his hands and swallowed convulsively. "I owe Roman my life."

Budimir studied Vincent impassively. He could see why his grandson had become friends with the boy. He had guts.

Vincent cleared his throat. "Has there—has there been a ransom demand?"

"No." Budimir paused. "And I don't expect there will be one."

Vincent's figure shriveled as he sagged on the bed.

"I'm sorry," he whispered. "I thought Roman was joking when he told me about his magic." His breath hitched. "I never meant for any of this to happen." He cast a wild look at Budimir, tears glittering in his eyes. "You have to believe me!"

Budimir watched him for a silent moment.

"Anyone would assume the same upon hearing such an assertion, child," he finally said. "This might bring you little comfort, but I'm confident what happened had little to do with your choices, however regretful they were. Those men would have found Roman eventually."

Vincent sniffed and wiped his eyes with the back of a hand.

Budimir suddenly felt his age where he sat in the visitor's chair next to the bed. Regret crumpled his heart.

Was I wrong to stop Roman from using his powers?

The words of his dead wife echoed through his skull.

"Please, Budimir," she'd begged him on her death bed. "Promise me you'll keep Roman safe. You have to hide him, or they'll take him away and do God only knows what to him!"

Budimir ground his teeth. *Damn those Vissarions!*

Alas, it was thirty-three years too late to curse them. Though his wife Eleanora had told him about her family's extraordinary abilities when he'd decided to ask the Vissarions' matriarch for her hand in marriage, Budimir had not believed her. He'd assumed

Eleanora meant her family were into some kind of pagan ritual when she'd spoken about magic. As far as he'd been concerned, that kind of stuff didn't exist.

What a fool I was.

He still recalled the day Roman first manifested his Fire Magic with vivid clarity. The boy had been eight at the time. Eleanora had told Budimir it was the trauma of Roman losing his parents in a recent car accident that had triggered his magic core.

Budimir would never forget the terror that had filled his wife's face when she'd seen the rare and powerful ability their grandson had inherited from the Vissarion bloodline.

He'd known little about Katarina Vissarion, Eleanora's second cousin. Katarina and her brother Yuliy had attended their wedding and he'd worked alongside Yuliy through the Bratva he'd aligned himself with, but he'd never been close to them. It was only after Katarina's death that Eleanora had finally told Budimir the secrets she had long kept about the Vissarions. About how Katarina had been the most powerful fire witch to have ever been birthed in the world of magic and how the main Vissarion house had practically enslaved her with their lies so as to use and abuse her powers.

It was then that he'd understood why Yuliy, who'd come from immense wealth and privilege, had joined the Bratva at age eighteen. The only way he could remove his younger sister from the reach of their influential kin was by forging blood bonds with another equally powerful family.

Vincent's voice brought him back to the present.

"Zak and his friends. Are they really…gone?"

"Yes. They died of cyanide poisoning."

Vincent recoiled at his blunt answer. A bolt of pity shot through Budimir as he observed the boy's ashen face. The trauma of what he'd seen would likely live with him forever more.

Let's hope a day comes when he can forgive himself.

"I still can't believe it was real," Vincent murmured. "That— *magic* is real!"

Budimir pressed his hands on his knees and rose. "It would be best if you refrained from telling other people what you witnessed that night."

A bitter expression flitted across Vincent's face. "Don't worry. The cops and my family already think I'm crazy."

Budimir's tone softened a little. "They'll put it down to shock. Still, the less you talk about this, the better. Those men let you get away because they thought you didn't pose a threat to them. Make sure you keep it that way."

His bodyguards opened the door as he made to leave.

Budimir slowed to a stop on the threshold. He turned to cast a final look at the boy in the hospital bed. "If Roman makes it back alive, will you still be his friend?"

Vincent blinked.

"Of course!" he blurted out.

Budimir smiled. "Good. He needs people like you in his life."

He twisted on his heels and exited the room, his smile fading to a frown.

"Take me to the school," he told his guards brusquely.

Budimir stared blindly at the streets they passed on the way to the private institution Roman had attended. For the first time in his life, he felt at a loss. Human enemies he could deal with. He'd never had to face an adversary who possessed supernatural powers.

He clenched his jaw, the truth that had dawned upon him when he'd heard of the circumstances behind Roman's disappearance echoing through his gut. The injuries that had killed the bodyguards tasked with his grandson's safekeeping had not been caused by normal weapons.

I have to fight like with like. Which means I need to get in touch with him.

Something bitter swirled through Budimir when Vlad Vissarion's face rose before his mind's eye.

The police checked their license plate when they got to the school and let them through. Budimir was conscious of the eyes following him as he and his guards made their way through the dormitory to Roman's room.

None of the other dead boys' families had been allowed inside the building.

Then again, none of them have the city's deputy chief of police in their pocket.

Roman's room showed no signs of the search that had already been carried out by the detectives investigating his disappearance and the other boys' murders. Melancholy gripped Budimir as he walked around and touched his grandson's belongings, his fingers trailing over sports trophies and framed certificates of achievement.

Roman had been a stellar student who excelled in both academics and sports and was well liked by his teachers and classmates alike.

A small diary poking out from under the bed caught his eye. He frowned. It looked old, its pages curled from being leafed through repeatedly.

Budimir leaned down, picked it up, and opened it. His pulse stuttered when he saw the handwriting on the first page.

It belonged to his dead wife.

His heart thundered against his ribs as he thumbed rapidly through the journal. They were notes on magic.

It took him but an instant to realize Eleanora had left the diary to Roman before her death.

Budimir's fingers clenched on the journal.

He should have felt betrayed. Except he didn't.

He knew Roman was alive. He could feel it in his gut. And the only reason his grandson had survived the attack that had killed his classmates was because he'd been able to wield the powers Budimir had banned him from using. Powers he'd evidently been practicing in hiding using the information in the very diary Budimir now held.

He closed his eyes shakily.

Thank you, Eleanora! You must have had a premonition that he would need to use his magic to defend himself one day!

It wasn't until he got to the end of the journal that another of his wife's many secrets came to light. Budimir's eyes widened when he read the final inscription.

The knowledge imprinted upon the pages he held had not belonged to Eleanora Vissarion. She had, it seemed, only been a scribe.

Roman had learned how to apply his Fire Magic from the most powerful witch to have arisen from the Vissarion bloodline.

CHAPTER FOURTEEN

"Yeah, I'll bring souvenirs," Mae said morosely into her cell phone.

"Tell her to buy us some Stoodle!" Ye-Seul shouted in the background.

Mae grimaced. "Does she mean Strudel?"

"I think so," Yoo-Mi said acerbically. "You never know with your grandmother."

Mae sighed.

"Like I said, I'm sorry," she repeated for the tenth time. "I totally forgot."

"I get that!" Yoo-Mi snapped. There was a short silence. "I just—I'm worried about you."

Guilt pricked Mae's conscience at the way her mother's voice trembled. "I'll be alright, Mom. Besides, Violet and Miles are with me. And Vlad is here too."

"Oh." Yoo-Mi's voice brightened. "Vlad's with you? Put him on."

"He's not with me right now." Mae narrowed her eyes. "It irks me that you sound more pleased about the fact that the incubus is around than your own daughter telling you she's gonna be okay."

Yoo-Mi tsk-tsked. "At least he's a responsible young man. I bet *he* wouldn't forget to tell his mom—"

"Bless her soul," they both mumbled.

"—before he left town," Yoo-Mi finished stridently.

Mae looked at Brimstone where he rode beside her on the backseat of the limo. "I'm never gonna hear the end of this, am I?"

Brimstone huffed commiseratively.

"Put Noah on, will you?" Mae told her mother.

Noah Tegner, Bryony's nephew and the sorcerer in charge of the team tasked with keeping the Jins safe, came on the line.

"Hey, Mae. How's Prague?"

"Drizzly," Mae said sourly. "You better be careful. Mom's on a rampage. She might not be so forgiving if she catches you two in the act."

There was a short lull.

"I'm not quite sure what you mean," Noah said carefully.

Mae sighed. "I know you and Ryu are playing hide the salami. You guys need to pipe down. I barely got any sleep the last time I stayed over, what with all the grunting and moaning." She paused, her brow furrowing. "Appearances really are deceptive. I would never have put you down as a depraved beast in the bedroom."

Noah sucked in air.

Mae ended the call and faced Miles and Violet's grins.

"Noah and Ryu finally did the dirty?" Miles said.

"That guy's a demon," Mae grumbled. "My sister is gonna need stamina pills."

The stone towers of a granite bridge appeared at the end of the avenue. The limo Marlena had sent to collect them from the airport took the exit on the left before they reached it. A dark, wooded island loomed out of the river ahead of them. It was connected to the city by a barrier-controlled overpass.

They crossed over and headed for a track that carved between the towering evergreens. It soon became a graveled driveway. Victorian lampposts appeared, the bulbs casting a soft, golden glow onto the pale stones. The aspect opened up after some three hundred feet.

Mae's pulse quickened as she stared at the imposing, double-winged, Neo-Gothic mansion looming out of the center of an expansive, manicured garden. They pulled into the front courtyard of the building a moment later.

Light rain peppered Mae's face as she stepped out of the vehicle with Brimstone. She looked up at a complex facade brimming with gargoyles rising under an overcast night sky.

"I don't know why, but I half expected the Council of the Moon's headquarters to be all white and church-like and stuff," Miles muttered as he and Violet joined her.

"You mean, instead of Dracula's summer home?" Violet said wryly.

Apprehension oozed through Mae as they climbed

the steps to the porch and a pair of striking, iron-studded doors. She could sense Nikolai and Alastair's cores in the distance.

There was something...different about the energy they were emitting.

Marlena met them in the main hall, her footsteps echoing on the mosaic floor and around the cavernous vestibule and her terrier trotting beside her.

Her voice shook with relief as she hugged Mae. "I'm glad you made it safely."

Mae squeezed her tightly before stepping back and scanning her face. "How is he?"

"He's pretty much recovered from what happened," Marlena said in clipped tones. "He's just..." Her voice trailed off. "It's better if you see for yourself." She rubbed her forehead tiredly. "It's kinda hard to explain."

Mae exchanged a worried glance with Violet and Miles. Dread trailed cold fingers down her spine as they headed deeper into the building with Marlena. Murmurs followed them, the sorcerers and witches they crossed paths with goggling openly at Mae and Brimstone.

"I'm sorry," Marlena said with a grimace. "They kinda heard you were coming."

The eerie energy Mae had sensed from Nikolai's core grew stronger when they took the stairs to a basement. They negotiated a series of shadowy corridors and approached a room at the end of a wide passage.

The double doors were protected by spells erected

by a group of sorcerers and witches. Mae examined the multi-layered shield curiously.

The pale wall throbbed with Moon Magic.

She would have taken a closer look under different circumstances.

"Let us through," Marlena commanded.

The magic users withdrew their guards, their gazes widening in recognition as they registered Mae and Brimstone's presence.

Marlena opened the doors without preamble and entered the chamber beyond. Mae followed and froze a few steps inside. Violet gasped beside her. Miles swore.

Brimstone grew alert next to Mae, his curiosity evident.

Goosebumps broke out across her skin despite the heat washing over her. She stared, her heart in her mouth.

Nikolai and Alastair stood facing a red chameleon in the middle of a large, circular, sunken floor enclosed by a veritable cage of shields.

All three were on fire.

It took but a moment for Mae to realize that the makeshift magic prison they stood inside was the only thing stopping the violent power spewing from their cores from destroying the room and likely half the building. Faint cracks were already visible on the floor and walls, a zigzag pattern that radiated from the center of the chamber.

The faces of the sorcerers and witches maintaining the defensive shield were gaunt with exhaustion. Mae spotted another group sitting on the ground and realized they were taking turns maintaining the barrier.

"Calm down," Nikolai was telling the chameleon firmly. "We mean you no harm."

From the way a muscle danced in his cheek, Mae deduced he'd been trying to appease the creature for some time.

The lizard spit angrily, her tail snapping from side to side.

Brimstone's ears pricked. *She's a familiar.*

Mae swallowed. She could sense the creature's abject fear through her link with the fox.

Something else dawned on her. Something that had been nagging at her subconscious ever since she'd felt the weird power coming from Nikolai and Alastair. She met Brimstone's gaze, surprise reverberating through her.

"Is that—?!"

Yes.

Mae fisted her hands. She stormed across the floor, the fox at her side. Nikolai stiffened when he saw them. Relief brightened his eyes across the flames and the barrier separating them. Alastair welcomed Brimstone with a flap of his fiery wings.

"Mae!"

Another emotion choked the sorcerer's throat as his gaze roamed her face. Her heart swelled at what she read in his eyes.

"Drop the barrier," she told Marlena over her shoulder.

"What?" Marlena's expression grew strained. "But

it's the only thing stopping this building's foundations from collapsing!"

Mae's gaze locked with Nikolai's. "I'll shield them."

Marlena hesitated.

"Do as she says," she told the witches and sorcerers at her command reluctantly.

They shot nervous glances at one another before bobbing their heads. Heat warmed Mae's blood as she reached for her magic.

"Now," she ordered grimly.

She raised a hand and silently invoked the spell just as the Council of the Moon's shields started winking out.

Contain.

A crimson bubble replaced the vanishing barrier. The sorcerers and witches fell back with startled cries as it expanded and filled half the room.

"Wait. Was that a wordless incantation?!"

Violet's stunned voice reached Mae dimly where she stood within the protective sphere.

"You came," Nikolai whispered.

Mae closed the distance to the sorcerer, clasped his face, and kissed him. He gasped, his fear echoing through her as his flames engulfed her too.

He wrenched his mouth from hers and tried to push her away.

"Wait! You don't know what this could do to you!"

"Relax," Mae murmured. "It won't hurt me."

Brimstone shifted into his nine-tailed fox-demon form, flipped the outraged chameleon onto her back, and pressed a giant paw lightly upon her belly.

"*Calm down, lizard,*" he growled inches from her face.

The chameleon hiccupped and went limp. The fire surrounding her winked out.

"You didn't kill her, did you?" Mae asked worriedly.

Brimstone let out a sigh that rattled the chandeliers. "*Of course not.*"

Mae gasped when Nikolai's mouth landed on hers. The blaze engulfing him and Alastair had receded. She responded to his touch and his lips with equal passion as he took her in his hold, her own arms locking tightly around his neck.

It wasn't until someone cleared their throat loudly that she realized she was riding his thigh with her leg and that his hands were under her T-shirt.

"We should have recorded this and sent it to Vlad," Violet told Miles.

Mae and Nikolai unlocked lips stiffly and stepped away from one another under a battery of avid stares. Hellreaver wheezed where he lay against her breastbone.

Holy Hellfire! I thought I was a goner there. What with your boobs and his chest, I swear I saw the pearly ga—!

Mae muzzled him with one hand.

A man built like a tank and sporting a hawk on his wrist entered the chamber. A faint frown marred his brow as he rotated his right shoulder with a distracted expression.

"Alright, I'm all rested and ready to—" He froze when he saw Mae and Brimstone. Pale magic bloomed on his fingertips as he assumed a defensive stance. "What the—?!"

Klara appeared behind him, her ferret clinging to her shoulders. She rocked to a halt when she saw Mae.

Her face crumpled. "Thank God!"

"Put that away," Marlena snapped at the Tank, indicating his magic.

Her terrier huffed.

CHAPTER FIFTEEN

"Hellfire?" Nikolai said numbly.

"Yeah. The flames you manifested carry the same energy signature as the portal Brimstone came to Earth through." Mae faltered. "It can't hurt me, since I have demonic power in my core."

They had relocated to Marlena's office, on the second floor of the mansion. Julius Vlach was sitting as far away from Brimstone as he could and kept glancing anxiously at his hawk where the latter was calmly grooming the fur between the nine-tailed fox's ears.

All the familiars in the room had gathered on and around the demonic spirit.

"Is it me or does that look like a scene from some ghoulish version of *Bambi*?" Miles muttered to Violet.

The witch grimaced. Her rabbit Trixie had draped herself across one of Brimstone's giant knuckles like some kind of sacrificial offer and was snoring softly, a hind leg twitching from time to time.

Marlena stared from Nikolai to Mae, pale-faced.

"I've never heard of a human being able to manipulate the fires of Hell."

"It's called Hellfire Magic, to be precise. Azazel was the one who created it."

Marlena and Klara startled as Brimstone's voice rattled the windows.

Julius's eyes bulged.

"He can talk?!" the sorcerer whispered fiercely to Violet.

"Yeah. Don't worry, it soon gets old."

Mae's pulse quickened. "Wait. Does that mean I can use this magic too?"

"Probably. Although I think Eclipse *is just as effective."*

"What the heck is Hellfire Magic anyway?" Miles asked.

"It is a power akin to Heaven's Fire," Brimstone replied. *"Only a few archangels are able to wield it. Azazel was one of them. He used Heaven's Fire to design Hellfire Magic."* The fox's expression turned brooding. *"Heaven's Fire is an unimaginable, destructive force that has wiped out entire worlds in the past. So is its derivative, Hellfire Magic. Azazel was so wary of what he'd created, he sealed it somewhere secret."*

Miles blinked rapidly. He turned to Violet. "Artemus's flames. I wonder if that's Heaven's Fire!"

Mae frowned faintly. Artemus Steele was a Chicago ally she had yet to meet but had heard much about. The son of an archangel, he was the leader of a group of beings destined to defend mankind in the holy war at the End of Days, just as she apparently was too.

"Does Fire Magic have anything to do with Hellfire Magic?" Nikolai asked Brimstone.

His face was haggard with dread. Mae had an inkling what was eating at the sorcerer. It was the same fear gnawing at her insides.

If Hellfire Magic was indeed that powerful, then Vedran and the Dark Council had even more reason to get their hands on him now.

"They have common elements. But they are different entities."

Julius stirred. "Nikolai already has Moon Magic and white magic, which is rare enough in itself." The sorcerer frowned. "How on earth did he acquire Hellfire Magic?"

Nikolai's gaze found the chameleon lying motionless on her back on the floor in front of Brimstone. "She had something to do with it. She was —hidden inside the nexus beneath this mansion. I tapped into her magic when I accessed a ley line during our training."

Everyone stared at the chameleon. She twitched slightly.

Brimstone lowered his head and huffed out smoke trails over her still form. *"We know you're awake, lizard."*

The chameleon flipped herself onto her front, her casque quivering.

"You're scaring her," Mae admonished.

"I can't help it." Brimstone sniffed. *"She reminds me of an annoying dragon I used to know."*

The lizard tasted the air carefully with her tongue. She rolled an eye at Mae and crossed the room toward her. Mae startled when the creature climbed her leg and settled on her lap.

"Get away from my witch, lizard!" Brimstone growled.

Hellreaver vibrated against her chest, similarly annoyed.

Mae ignored them and petted the familiar. "There, there. I won't let those big meanies hurt you."

The chameleon huddled in on herself before nudging Mae's palm gently with her head. She made a happy sound.

"Can you talk to her?" Mae asked Brimstone.

"Do I have to?" the fox asked sullenly.

Mae narrowed her eyes.

"Alright, alright," Brimstone grumbled. *"Hey, lizard, what's your name?"*

The creature twisted around to face the fox. Soft clicks left her throat.

"She says her name is Filomena." Brimstone cocked his head to the side, his pupils constricting. *"She and her sorcerer were...attacked, a couple of days ago."* The fox's ears flicked forward and backward in surprise. *"She says he saved her by teleporting her to the nexus."*

The hairs on Mae's nape rose at the ramifications of that statement.

The meaning behind Brimstone's words wasn't lost on Nikolai either. The sorcerer had gone deathly still.

"Wait!" Violet gasped. "That would make her sorcerer a ley-line user too!"

Marlena's eyes rounded. Julius cursed.

"She says she and her sorcerer are—" Brimstone paused,

his pupils dilating. He cast a somber glance at Mae. *"She says they're Fire Magic users and that they were targeted because of their powers."* His face darkened. *"She says she's afraid the men who took her master will kill him soon."*

"Fire Magic users?" Mae repeated, stunned.

She stared at the chameleon.

Filomena had turned to look at her. She whimpered.

Mae clenched her jaw.

"What is it?" Nikolai said stiffly. His gaze swung from Mae to Violet and Miles's troubled expressions. "Do you know something about what happened to them?"

Mae dipped her head. "Not them per se. But I think the Dark Council is targeting Fire Magic users for one of their schemes."

She gave them the lowdown on the dead witches and sorcerer she had recently examined in New York and Salem.

"The Dark Council killed them?!" Marlena said, aghast.

A whine escaped her familiar.

Julius was scowling. "Their cores imploded?"

"Yeah. And there are three still missing." Mae cast an apologetic look at Nikolai. "I didn't want to burden you when we spoke last. You had enough on your plate as it was." She hesitated as she studied the sorcerer's ashen complexion. "Do you have any idea what Vedran and Oscar might be up to?"

Nikolai swallowed and shook his head. "I haven't

heard anything from my contacts. They must be keeping whatever this is close to their chest."

He hesitated.

Mae reached over and placed her hand atop the back of his. "What is it?"

Nikolai shuddered and turned his palm over. He linked his fingers with hers and met her gaze. "I sensed something strange when I accessed the nexus. Something that felt…wrong, the more I think about it now."

Mae grew still. "Wrong how?"

"I think there might be a crack in the core of the nexus," Nikolai said grimly. "And if that crack expands, all Hell will break loose in this city."

CHAPTER SIXTEEN

Vlad frowned at his phone where he stood drying his hair with a towel in the middle of his hotel suite.

His contacts in Prague still hadn't located Budimir Volkov.

Where the hell did that old bastard go?

He checked his messages. Mae hadn't been in touch since they'd parted ways at the airport either. He'd booked her a suite opposite his and knew she hadn't arrived at the hotel yet.

He was brooding over what she was up to and whether she was still with Nikolai when a knock came at his door. Tarang opened a lazy eye where he lay on the couch and closed it again.

Seeing as how relaxed his familiar looked, Vlad gathered there wasn't an assassin outside his room intent on putting a bullet in his heart. He crossed the floor, looked into the peep hole, and sighed.

What now?

He opened the door to find Cortes standing in front of his room with a brooding expression.

"You'll be the first to know when I find Budimir," Vlad told the Colombian bluntly.

Cortes brushed past him and entered the suite. "That's not why I'm here."

"Come on in," Vlad said drily.

He looked out into the corridor, clocked Cortes's bodyguards chatting with Ilya and Milo, and closed the door. Cortes had made his way to the bar and was pouring himself a drink.

He shook a bottle of vodka at Vlad. "Want one?"

"Why not?"

He perched on a stool as the Colombian poured a second glass. Silence befell them as they drank.

"So, are you going to tell me why you're here or am I going to have to guess?" Vlad glanced at the sumptuous, king-size bed visible through the archway to his left. "FYI, if it's for a quick tumble between the sheets, I'm afraid my heart and my body belong to the Witch Queen."

Cortes curled his lip. "You're not my type." Lines wrinkled his brow. "It's about the compensation. I've changed my mind."

Vlad blinked, nonplussed. "What?"

"Forget about introducing me to Budimir."

Vlad's gut tightened. He didn't like the sound of where this was going.

"What do you mean?" he asked coldly.

"I want Mae to fix my core," Cortes said brusquely.

Vlad's eyes shrank to slits. "Come again?"

"You heard what she said on the plane." A muscle ticked in Cortes's jawline. "I have too much to accomplish still. I can't afford to die yet."

Anger quickened Vlad's pulse. He hated that everyone wanted to take advantage of his relationship with Mae to use her.

First the Bratva and now him. I really do want to shoot this asshole now!

Tarang raised his head and looked at them warily.

Cortes noted the familiar's fresh interest. "I'm not asking for the impossible. If anyone can fix my core, she can." He shrugged. "If she can't, then so be it. I'll resign myself to my fate." A mocking sneer twisted the Colombian's mouth as he studied Vlad's scowl. "Face it, if you were in my shoes, you'd be asking for the exact same thing."

Vlad's knuckles whitened on his glass. Cortes was right and they both knew it.

A commotion outside the suite had them both staring at the door.

Tarang jumped down from the couch and growled.

A knife appeared in Cortes's hand. A crimson aura detonated around Vlad.

The door clattered open. Ilya, Milo, and Cortes's men spilled into the room backward, their expressions tense and their weapons pointed at the floor.

Budimir Volkov and his bodyguards followed.

Vlad's heartbeat accelerated as he met the Bratva general's flinty gaze.

"We need to talk," Budimir said coldly.

Mae nearly dislocated her jaw as she yawned behind her hand.

Nikolai looked over from the driver's seat. He was taking Mae, Violet, and Miles to their hotel. "You could have stayed with Marlena and Klara."

"Vlad said he'd already booked us rooms."

She stroked Brimstone absentmindedly where he slept on her lap. Filomena was snoozing on the fox's head. The two familiars appeared to have reached some kind of truce.

Nikolai frowned. He hated the fact that Mae and Vlad would be sleeping in proximity to one another.

"Why aren't you staying with your family?"

He startled at her question and turned his head to meet her inquisitive stare. He was about to give her a pretext when Alastair clicked his beak.

The crow evidently didn't approve of him lying to the witch.

"I felt more comfortable in the dormitory," Nikolai finally confessed. "And I…don't know how to act around them."

"You don't trust them," Mae said shrewdly.

Nikolai blinked. A faint smile curved his lips.

Funny how she can see straight through me.

"There's also the library at the headquarters. I can go there anytime." His tone brightened. "The texts the Council of the Moon have about magic are new to me. I've learned a lot from—" He paused at her grin. "What?"

"Don't let Vlad hear you sound so enthusiastic about a bunch of books," Mae drawled. "He'd totally tease you."

"Yeah," Violet muttered from the backseat. "You'd never hear the end of it."

Nikolai's mood darkened again at the mention of the incubus. "What's he doing in Prague anyway?"

"He's here on business." Mae made a face. "You won't guess who's with him."

Nikolai shot her a wary look. "Who?"

"Vasco Gomez's boss."

Nikolai's hands nearly slipped off the steering wheel. "You mean the head of the *Bacatá Cartel?!*"

"Future head," Mae said. "He's an…interesting man."

Nikolai studied her pensive expression. Jealousy stabbed through him, cooling his tone. "Interesting how?"

"He's a magic user. But he has a cracked core."

Nikolai's eyes rounded. "What?"

Miles was staring out his window. "I think you just missed our hotel."

Nikolai swore and slammed on the brakes. Mae cursed when the seatbelt snapped into her midriff. Brimstone fell into the footwell and woke up with a growl. Filomena patted his head urgently with her feet to calm him down.

Horns blared behind them.

"Sorry."

Nikolai did an illegal U-turn and parked outside their hotel a moment later. Mae's cell rang just as he switched off the engine.

She dug her phone out from the back pocket of her jeans, took one look at the caller ID, and stiffened. She cast a furtive look at him before taking the call.

"What's up?" She paused. "I just got here." She frowned, shifted slightly toward the door, cupped her mouth with her hand, and hissed, "Seriously? No, I can't come to your room!"

Nikolai scowled. It didn't take a genius to figure out who'd rung her. He snatched her phone from her grasp.

"It's one o'clock in the morning, asshole!" he barked into the cell. "She's going to bed!"

Muffled swearing came from the speakers. Mae retrieved the device with a faint look of guilt.

"Nikolai is right, Vlad," she said with a sigh once she put her phone back to her ear. "Why don't we talk tomorrow? There's a lot we need to catch up—" Mae froze. Her eyes rounded. "What?!"

Nikolai tensed. Brimstone's ears perked up.

Mae's face tightened. "We'll be there in five." She disconnected and directed a somber stare at Nikolai. "You'd better come with us."

CHAPTER SEVENTEEN

Mae's tension ratcheted up another notch when she stepped out of the hotel elevator with Nikolai and the Nolan cousins. A group of dark-suited men stood outside Vlad's suite.

It was hard to miss their deadly expressions and the bulge of guns under their armpits.

"How come there's more of you every time I see you guys?" Mae asked Ilya and Milo glumly as she made her way over.

Ilya glanced at the four men Mae didn't recognize.

"They work for the main Bratva," he said guardedly.

Mae's scalp prickled when she registered the guards' stony faces. Cortes's men seemed equally uncomfortable in the presence of the newcomers.

She straightened her shoulders and rapped her knuckles on the door of Vlad's room.

It opened seconds later. Mae took one look at Vlad's distracted expression and knew this was going to be even worse than she'd thought. The incubus was slightly disheveled, like he'd dressed hurriedly.

"Come in," he said crisply.

She read the warning in his eyes and brushed past him, Nikolai, Violet, and Miles close on her heels. Vlad closed the door behind them.

Tarang looked over briefly from where he sat on the floor, facing a couch where two men sat. The tiger focused his attention on Vlad's guests once more, his blue eyes shrinking to watchful slits.

One of them was Cortes.

The other was a silver-haired, middle-aged man who filled the room with an overwhelming presence. His dark eyes pinned Mae with an inscrutable stare.

"Mae, this is Budimir Volkov," Vlad said in a clipped voice. "He's a senior member of the Bratva the *Black Devils* work for."

Mae's nails dug into her palms. *Shit! No wonder you could cut the air with a knife.*

Vlad introduced Nikolai and the Nolan cousins to his guests. A soft hiss escaped Filomena where she perched on Brimstone's head. Her casque quivered.

The chameleon was staring intently at Budimir.

Mae frowned. *Does she know him?*

Brimstone listened to Filomena's soft clicks. *It seems so.*

Mae observed the older man before directing a tense look at Vlad. "You said something about Oscar."

Nikolai startled. "What?!"

Vlad ran a hand through his hair and sighed heavily. "Play it again."

Budimir leaned forward. Mae noticed a damaged cell phone on the coffee table in front of him for the first time. Budimir entered a code and tapped the cracked screen. A recording started to play. Though the quality wasn't the best, she could make out most of the details.

Mae's eyes rounded.

"*Ignite!*" a male voice she didn't recognize shouted.

The stranger sounded young.

A violent thump echoed from the cell's speakers. The crackle of an intense blaze followed.

The voice that spoke next sent a chill down Mae's spine and drew a curse from Nikolai.

"Impressive," Oscar Beneventi drawled.

Filomena started trembling violently.

Mae and the others listened grimly as the sounds of an intense battle unfolded between Oscar and the younger man over several minutes. The last person who spoke was Oscar.

"*Disperse!*"

An explosion followed his spell. The recording ended soon after.

A strained silence ensued.

"The boy you just heard is Roman, my grandson," Budimir said in a voice underscored with steel. "He and his friends were attacked by a pair of magic users in this city, two nights ago. Five of them died. Roman managed to save his best friend before he was captured." Rage flickered briefly in the older man's eyes before he regained his iron composure once more. "We found his cell phone among the trees in the park where they were ambushed. The bodies of the guards I had assigned to his protection were discovered not far from where he disappeared."

A singular truth resonated through Mae as she met Budimir's gaze. "Roman has Fire Magic."

Budimir went deathly still at her quiet statement.

"How do you know that?" he asked in a dangerous tone.

"What?" Vlad had gone pale. His expression turned accusing as he looked from Mae to Budimir. "Is Mae right?!"

Surprise widened Mae's eyes. She'd rarely seen the incubus so upset.

She recalled his strange reluctance when he'd heard about the dead witch she'd examined, back when they'd had dinner at her apartment.

Budimir's face grew shuttered. "She is. It seems the Vissarions' Fire Magic skipped a single generation this time."

Mae stared at Vlad, her heart thumping wildly. "Your family are Fire Magic users?!"

Bitterness tightened Vlad's face. "My mother was the most powerful Fire Magic witch who ever lived."

Nikolai sucked in air.

Violet glanced at an equally stunned Miles. "How—how come we didn't know this?!"

"The Vissarions aren't famed for their openness." Vlad clenched his jaw. "That family is a nest of rats!"

"On that at least we concur," Budimir said darkly. He narrowed his eyes at Mae. "You still haven't answered my question, young lady."

Mae blinked at his polite address. Hellreaver snickered.

She shot a frown at the weapon before addressing the mobster. "It seems the Dark Council is actively hunting Fire Magic users."

She told them about the incidents in the U.S. and her findings when she'd examined the bodies of the three dead Fire Magic users she'd come across.

Cortes arched an eyebrow. "Their blood boiled in their veins?"

Mae nodded. "That's what it looked like. It must have happened when their cores imploded. Which makes sense considering their magic."

Budimir's knuckles whitened. "Why are they killing Fire Magic users?"

"I don't believe their primary intention was to kill them. I think they were intending to use them for something. That's why they went after your grandson." Mae paused, unease gnawing at her insides. "If Roman is as powerful as I think he is, then Oscar and Vedran just hit the jackpot."

A stilted silence befell them.

Budimir finally stirred. He leaned his elbows on his knees, his expression deadly. "Tell me more about these men."

Cortes listened just as attentively while Mae, Nikolai, Vlad, and the Nolan cousins recounted what they knew about the Sorcerer King and what had happened in New York and Philadelphia following Mae's awakening.

"You're the daughter of a fallen archangel turned

demon?" Budimir asked guardedly, appraising Mae with fresh eyes.

She wrinkled her nose. "Well, technically, I'm Na Ri's reincarnation. Brimstone and Hellreaver were originally intended to be hers."

Budimir gave her a blank look. "Brimstone and Hellreaver?"

"Oh." Mae blinked. "I guess you can't see them."

The familiars in the room manifested their presence. Budimir drew a sharp breath as he observed the creatures who'd been hidden from his sight. His gaze landed on Tarang.

"So, this is your infamous beast," he muttered, his expression unfathomable.

Vlad stepped defensively in front of the tiger.

Mae traded a puzzled glance with Nikolai.

Budimir stilled when Brimstone and Hellreaver transformed.

Cortes similarly stiffened.

It was the Colombian's first time seeing Brimstone's nine-tailed form.

"Mind the lights," Mae warned as the fox's enormous head brushed the ceiling.

"*I know,*" Brimstone grunted. He curled up on the floor, his tails thumping against furniture. "*Human homes could do with being bigger. The caves in Hell were far more comfortable.*"

Mae rolled her eyes.

Cortes was frowning at Filomena. "That one doesn't appear to have a master."

"She does." Mae looked at Budimir. "She's Roman's familiar."

CHAPTER EIGHTEEN

The old man blinked. "What?"

Filomena dropped down from Brimstone and approached the mobster, her tongue darting out to taste the air. She hesitated before climbing his leg and settling on his lap. A happy sound left her.

Budimir froze, his expression that of a man holding a bomb.

Cortes stared. "Wait. Are you scared of lizards?"

Everyone goggled at Budimir.

"I am not scared of them," the mobster said gruffly.

Mae grimaced. "Yeah, you are. She won't bite. Besides, you've probably been around her plenty of times before and never known it."

Budimir frowned. He raised a hand and touched Filomena hesitantly. The chameleon changed color, her casque quivering.

Budimir snatched his hand away. "What's happening?"

"*Relax,*" Brimstone said. "*She likes you.*"

Cortes looked like he was trying not to smile.

"There's something I don't get." Vlad lowered his brows. "How come she wasn't captured along with Roman?"

Mae looked at Nikolai. "It's better if you explain this part."

Dread clouded Vlad's face as the sorcerer told him and his guests what had happened during his training and the eerie power he now harbored.

"Hellfire Magic?" the incubus repeated numbly.

Mae's pulse quickened when she felt Nikolai draw on his new magic. The threads of energy resonating from his core called to her insidiously as they pulsed in tandem with her own demonic power.

Budimir and Cortes's eyed widened as Alastair's wings caught fire and a sphere of dark, crimson flames burst into life above Nikolai's hand.

"Wait." Vlad blinked when the truth struck him. "So, Roman can access ley lines too?!"

Nikolai retracted his Hellfire Magic. "Yes. That's how he managed to hide Filomena in the nexus."

Budimir scanned their uneasy faces. "This…ley line business. It sounds like the ability to use them is rare."

"It is," Mae said grimly. "Nikolai is—*was* the only magic user we knew of who could access the immense magic within the Earth. The Dark Council will do anything to get their hands on that kind of power."

Budimir looked old all of a sudden. "Does that mean they will try to use Roman in a similar fashion?"

"Only if they know about it." Nikolai was frowning.

"It isn't evident from what we just heard whether Oscar realized what Roman had done."

Mae lowered her brows. "I agree." She turned to Vlad. "Brimstone believes Fire Magic and Hellfire Magic have common elements." She hesitated. "Do you know much about Fire Magic?"

Vlad shook his head, his expression turning bitter. "I'm afraid not. Yuliy refused to talk about it for the most part. All he ever said was that the power my mother was born with was a curse, not a gift." His pupils flashed crimson at the same time a red haze bloomed around him. He stared at his left hand and slowly flexed his fingers. "Yuliy always wondered whether my incubus blood is the reason I didn't inherit her magic."

"He is right," Brimstone said. *"Your incubus energy and magic are incompatible with Fire Magic. It would make harboring it in your core extremely difficult."*

"Your mother's powers were only a curse because the Vissarions made it so," Budimir told Vlad curtly. "It seemed she knew this too."

Vlad flinched. "What do you mean?"

Budimir watched him for a beat before removing a small journal from inside his suit jacket. It was old, with yellowed, curled pages. He placed it on the table.

"Katarina Vissarion left a journal with her cousin Eleanora, my wife. In it are instructions on how to use Fire Magic and the spells Katarina herself had come up with. It was clear she intended for this knowledge to be passed on to the next most powerful Fire Magic user to be born from the Vissarion bloodline." He frowned.

"She must have known that wouldn't be you, or she would have left this with Yuliy for safekeeping."

Mae's pulse raced as she stared at the diary.

Vlad hesitated before walking over to the table and reaching for it. His fingers trembled as he opened the pages.

"Your mother would not have done this if she believed her magic was a curse," Budimir said. "Eleanora gave Katarina's journal to Roman before her death. It seems my grandson has been practicing his Fire Magic in secret all along." He paused. "And he learned it from the best."

Filomena clicked her tongue in agreement.

Vlad swallowed convulsively, his eyes dark with emotion. Tarang huffed and came over to brush his body against the incubus's legs.

Nikolai was studying Filomena with a faint frown. "There's one thing I still don't understand. Why did Roman hide Filomena in the nexus?"

"That should be obvious to all of you," Brimstone said in the puzzled silence.

Mae stared at the fox. Understanding dawned.

Her mouth rounded on a surprised "Oh!"

"Separating a familiar from his magic user weakens the latter's magic," Cortes said in a clipped tone. *"Killing their familiar will weaken their core enough for it to crack."*

Violet drew a sharp breath. Miles paled, his hand automatically finding Millie.

Mae's stomach twisted. "Is that how your aunt damaged your core?"

Cortes bobbed his head. "Roman is a smart kid. By physically distancing himself from his familiar, not only did he stop her from becoming a pawn his kidnappers could blackmail him with, but he also weakened his own magic."

Mae's heart slammed against her ribs. "Which means whatever Oscar and Vedran want to achieve through him is going to be that much harder to do!"

Brimstone made an approving sound.

"He bought himself time." Admiration brightened Vlad's gaze. "That's one genius move."

"How did the Dark Council find your grandson?" Cortes asked Budimir.

Budimir furrowed his brow. "His best friend told someone about his magic. But I suspect they were already looking for him."

"Not many people knew about the three suspected Fire Magic users who went missing last month either," Mae said slowly, her mind racing. "They never registered their ability with their covens. Could the Dark Council have found a way to identify and trace the location of Fire Magic users?"

"*I doubt Barquiel or that Immortal lackey of his possess such knowledge,*" Brimstone grumbled.

The blood suddenly drained from Nikolai's face. "Shit."

Alarm clenched Mae's belly. "What?"

"The seer." He met her gaze wildly. "I forgot about her!"

Mae blinked. She scowled as she recalled what Nikolai had told her the first time they'd spoken with

Bryony. "You mean the one who foresaw my awakening?"

Nikolai nodded numbly. "There's a strong possibility Raya is using her powers to identify Fire Magic users."

"What…did you just say?!" someone choked out.

Mae's head whipped around.

Cortes had risen to his feet. A thunderous expression darkened his face. "The name. What's the name of this—seer?!"

"Raya Medeiros," Nikolai replied, confused.

Cortes closed his eyes and shuddered. The bloodlust that filled his gaze when he opened them again gave Mae the answer she was looking for.

"Is she the one who damaged your core?!" she gasped.

Vlad and Nikolai cast shocked looks at Cortes. Surprise flitted across Budimir's face.

"Yes." A muscle jumped in the Colombian's jawline. "She's my aunt." Cortes's gaze locked on Mae. "Let me help you. I may not be able to use my magic, but I have contacts on this continent who can find Raya now that I know she's close. In exchange, I want you to fix my core."

Mae startled. "What?"

"I also have a request." Budimir's gaze swept the room before focusing on her. "I want you to help me save Roman."

CHAPTER NINETEEN

A WOMAN'S SCREAM JOLTED ROMAN OUT OF HIS FITFUL slumber. He bolted upright, his heart slamming against his ribs. His fingers dug convulsively into the thin pallet he lay upon as his gaze swept his prison wildly, his vision already accustomed to the gloom.

It was empty but for the bare, stone walls surrounding him on three sides and the faint light coming from a flame torch in the corridor outside. Roman swallowed, braced his hands on the ground, and rose. A few steps took him to the iron grille making up the fourth wall and door. He peered outside, careful not to touch metal.

It was infused with black magic and had already scorched his palms once.

"It's Laura," a voice quavered in the darkness.

Roman's gaze found the pale face staring out of another cell across the way. Both he and the man jumped when another scream came from somewhere in the distance. It faded into a long, low moan of agony.

Anger and fear surged through Roman.

It had been two days since he'd woken up in this hellish place. He'd been shocked to discover there were other prisoners in the dungeon where the men who had attacked him had brought him. His worst fears had been realized when they'd told him they were Fire Magic users too and apprised him of what had been happening down there.

There had been even more sorcerers and witches in the prison before he came. One, sometimes two people were dragged from their cell every day, never to return.

Roman didn't have to be a genius to figure out the dreadful ending the missing magic users had met. From the bloodcurdling sounds he could hear coming from Laura wherever she had been taken to, the witch's fate had already been sealed.

He hadn't seen the red-haired sorcerer in the time he'd been down here. According to the other Fire Magic users, the guy's name was Oscar Beneventi. He was the son of the Sorcerer King and the one who would inherit his seat at the head of the Dark Council.

Even though Roman knew little of the current politics of the magic community, he'd read about the Dark Council and the Sorcerer King in Katarina Vissarion's journal. And he'd seen what Oscar Beneventi could do. Though he'd put up a valiant fight, it hadn't taken long for the sorcerer to overpower him with his black magic.

The one difference between him and the other Fire Magic users trapped alongside him, and possibly his saving grace, was that his familiar hadn't been captured. Roman suspected Oscar Beneventi was still pissed about that fact.

He swallowed heavily. *I'm just glad Filomena is safe.*

Though they were physically apart, Roman could still sense his familiar faintly through the bond that linked their cores. He'd been worried when he'd felt her intense distress upon waking up in the cell where he'd been imprisoned. He knew the chameleon had been beyond upset that he'd sent her away.

He'd also been concerned about her fate.

Casting her into the nexus had been a last-ditch attempt to save them both. He hadn't known if she would be able to make her way out or if she would remain trapped down there. As a creature of magic, she would likely survive in that environment for some time.

The fact that her emotions had settled somewhat in the last day was only half reassuring. Roman fisted his hands.

I have to find a way out of here. I have to tell the Council of the Moon what's happening and save Filo!

Though he'd never interacted with the sorcerers and witches he knew to be in the city, it had been child's play guessing where their headquarters was. He'd spent plenty of time on the bridge that overlooked the island where he'd sensed a concentration of strong magic, watching the vehicles that drove in and out of the woods.

A dog's tortured howl raised goosebumps on Roman's flesh. Laura screamed again.

It sounded like they were ripping her limbs apart.

Bile rose in Roman's throat. He pressed a hand to his mouth and gagged. Whimpers of terror sounded from the cells around him.

Laura and her familiar went quiet.

Roman shuddered. He stumbled to a stone wall, pressed his back against it, and slid down onto his bottom. He hugged his legs to his chest and choked back tears, knowing he would never see the witch or her dog again.

He didn't know how long he'd been sitting like that for when an eerie pressure somewhere in the dungeon made his ears pop. The air grew heavy and oily.

Roman's eyes widened. He scrambled to his feet and backed up to the far corner of his cell. He could feel someone approaching. Someone whose energy made his stomach roil.

The sound of heels clacking against stone rose from the corridor.

The other sorcerer and witches had similarly moved away from their doors and were crouching in the shadows of their prisons with their familiars. They'd warned him about the person he suspected was coming down the passage. Roman swallowed.

Though she's not exactly a person.

A figure appeared in front of his cell. He stared.

A tall, pretty blonde with gray eyes stood watching him steadily through the bars.

"You must be the boy who upset Oscar," she drawled.

Roman fisted his hands. Despite the stranger's beauty, he knew he was looking at a monster.

The blonde narrowed her eyes at his silence. "Come here."

Roman stood his ground and glared at her.

The blonde tsk-tsked. She raised a hand and curled her index finger.

A gasp left him when an invisible force squeezed his arms and legs together and dragged him across the floor. Roman clenched his teeth as he came to a jarring stop a mere inch from the metal grille. His pulse raced.

The black magic coating the iron bars washed across his flesh in corrupt trails he couldn't see but could feel with every fiber of his being.

Crimson flashed in the blonde's eyes. She smiled and cocked her head. "Don't worry. I would never spoil a pretty face like yours."

Roman shuddered as she reached through the bars and danced a nail down his cheek. She leaned in and scented the air around him, like a predator savoring her prey.

"Hmm, the sweet smell of a virgin." She licked her lips. "I may have to ask Oscar if he wouldn't mind me breaking you in before he gets on with the business he has with you."

Revulsion tightened Roman's jaw at her sick suggestion. His skin crawled when she straightened and scanned his body from head to toe.

"I doubt I'd get it up for you," he spat.

The blonde blinked at his words.

The air left his lungs the next instant as the force holding him prisoner flung him across the cell. Pain bloomed on his spine and across the back of his skull when he struck the wall hard. He thought he heard a rib snap.

Roman slumped to the ground, his legs tingling. Nausea churned his stomach as numbness gave way to agony. He swallowed a groan and shook his head dazedly.

Strike one for the demon.

Hysterical laughter choked his throat at that insane thought.

The blonde's voice reached him through the ringing in his ears.

"You have quite the smart mouth on you, kid," she said dispassionately. "Let's see how long you can keep it up for when I sink my claws into your core."

The cell door opened. A pair of blurry figures appeared. Cruel hands grabbed him by his arms and dragged him out of his prison.

Roman thought he heard the other Fire Magic users shout out his name as his knees scraped painfully across the uneven ground. His vision swam when he tried to make sense of where they were taking him. Stairs appeared, an endless flight of steps that bruised his shins. A door danced into view moments later.

It opened to reveal some kind of lab.

Movement captured his gaze as hands lifted him and dumped him roughly on a table. He barely noted the cold metal kissing his skin and the leather straps biting into his wrists and ankles as he stared at the body being wheeled away on a gurney.

It was Laura.

The witch's body was contorted in violent

contractions that had bent her spine, limbs, and even her jaw at impossible angles. Strange red lines were fading from her skin and her clawed fingers and toes were slowly relaxing.

A whimper left Roman when he saw her familiar where the latter's corpse was being disposed of in a bag. The dog was burned beyond recognition, his carcass all but a few scraps of blackened flesh and tendons clinging to charred bones.

Someone came inside the room. Roman's head spun as he turned it a fraction. A handsome man with fair hair and a lab coat stormed over to the blonde where she stood watching him with a callous expression.

"What are you doing, Barquiel?!" The stranger glanced at Roman, his gaze as cold and as unfeeling as the blonde's. "Oscar said we aren't to touch him until we've located his familiar. There's no point going for his core right now. He's too weak and he'll die without giving us what we want."

"I'm aware of that, Dietrich." The blonde's evil gaze found Roman. "But I can still play with him."

The guy called Dietrich glared at her before blowing out a frustrated sigh. "Oh, do what you want!" He threw his hands in the air and made for the exit, grumbling all the while. "You're the only one who can test Vedran's patience so, but even *he* will be pissed if you rob him of the chance to get his hands on Hellfire Magic!"

The door slammed closed after him.

Roman blinked. *Hellfire Magic?!*

The blonde approached the table. She leaned down

until her face was mere inches from his. His heart contracted with fear as he stared into her crimson pupils and smelled the corruption oozing from her flesh.

She smiled. "Any last words before I rake your internal organs with my nails?"

Roman swallowed. He raised his head.

"Yes," he whispered a hairbreadth from her lips.

Her pupils dilated and contracted, her interest piqued.

Roman bared his teeth. "Do your worst, demon."

The blonde's smile faded. He saw her fingers lengthen into dark talons out the corner of his eye. Then she punched her hand inside his belly in a move that should have been impossible.

Agony roared through Roman as a vile energy squeezed his core. He threw his head back and screamed.

CHAPTER TWENTY

"I killed Budimir's son," Vlad said quietly.

Mae's eyes rounded. Nikolai, Violet, and Miles stared, equally shocked.

Tarang pushed his head under Vlad's hand where he sat on the couch. A soft whine left the familiar. Vlad ran his fingers through the tiger's fur, grateful as ever for his comforting presence.

It was past three in the morning. Cortes and Budimir had left the suite a short while ago, with the promise to catch up with them in the morning.

Vlad's pulse thumped hard as he looked up into Mae's face. To his surprise, he didn't see the disgust he'd expected to find there. It gave him the courage to continue.

"Budimir had an illegitimate child with one of his prostitutes before he married Eleanora Vissarion. His name was Kaspar Petrovich. Kaspar was disowned by his father at a young age. Despite this, he still chose to join the Bratva Budimir worked for. I'm still not sure whether it was to spite him or gain his affection."

Mae rose from her chair and came over to sit next to him. She took his hand wordlessly, as if to give him strength to carry on talking.

Vlad inhaled raggedly, emotion tightening his throat. All the feelings and the madness of the terrible night that had changed his life forever crashed over him, emptying his lungs of air.

It was almost a minute before he could speak again.

"Kaspar rapidly went on to make a name for himself in the Bratva ranks, enough that his reputation brought him to Yuliy's attention after my uncle relocated to the U.S. and formed the *Black Devils* with the main syndicate's blessing. Yuliy eventually chose him as his heir and the next leader of our group."

"You mean, you were never meant to inherit his seat?" Nikolai said, startled.

Vlad shook his head. "Yuliy wanted me as far away from the Bratva as possible. He'd promised my mother he wouldn't let me enter a life of crime, like he'd been forced to."

Mae squeezed his fingers.

Anger stirred through Vlad as Kaspar's face rose before his eyes. "Had it not been for Kaspar's greed, he would still be alive today and I would be free of the shackles of the underworld."

"What did he do?" Mae asked.

Vlad swallowed. "He tried to kill Yuliy. He poisoned him, in fact."

Tension thickened the air.

"That's when you killed him?" Mae probed.

"It wasn't just him." A bitter chuckle left Vlad. "I lost control of my incubus powers and annihilated him and fifty of our followers who had chosen to betray my uncle and sworn their allegiance to him."

Nikolai drew a sharp breath.

Vlad shuddered. The scenes of gore and mayhem he'd woken to after the darkness within him had consumed his and Tarang's souls for those infinite minutes were imprinted in his mind for eternity.

They had only been able to identify the bodies from their dental records.

"The Bratva didn't punish you?" Nikolai said stiffly.

"No. Considering Kaspar almost killed Yuliy, my actions were justifiable."

"And Budimir just forgave you?" Mae asked skeptically.

"I...don't know," Vlad said truthfully.

Despite dozens of men witnessing him ripping Kaspar's heart from his chest with his bare hands, he had still not fathomed Volkov's feelings on the matter to this day. Was it honor and the Bratva code that had stopped the man from seeking revenge for his son's death? Or had he not cared for Kaspar at all?

"I did not sense any bloodlust from him during your interactions," Brimstone observed. *"Of course, if he does hold feelings of revenge toward you, they may be circumvented by his current desire to find his grandson."*

Vlad met Mae's gaze steadily.

"You don't owe Budimir anything." He cast an awkward glance at Nikolai and the Nolan cousins.

"Neither do you guys. You don't have to do what he's asking of you."

Mae sighed. "We don't really have a choice. This involves Oscar and the Dark Council. We can't let them carry on doing whatever they're planning to do with Fire Magic users." She glanced at Filomena where the familiar perched on the coffee table. "Besides, not helping her sorcerer would leave a bitter taste in my mouth."

"*I agree,*" Brimstone said.

Nikolai and the others dipped their chins.

"What about Cortes?" Vlad asked Mae guardedly. "Is what he's asking of you even possible?"

Lines wrinkled Mae's brow. "I'm not sure. But if anyone can fix his core, it's either me or Azazel."

Brimstone's ears pricked forward. Alastair squawked out a warning.

Filomena screeched, flipped onto her back, and started convulsing.

※

MAE JUMPED TO HER FEET, ALARM TWISTING HER GUT. She could sense something within the chameleon's core. Something that reeked of Hell's corruption.

"What's happening to her?!" Nikolai said.

"I don't know!"

The sorcerer moved to touch the familiar.

"*Don't,*" Brimstone warned. "*Her core is unstable!*"

As if to prove his point, flames detonated around Filomena.

Mae's eyes widened. *Her Fire Magic is out of control!*

She clenched her jaw, tapped into the power simmering inside her body, and raised a hand. "*Contain!*"

Her spell enclosed Filomena inside a barrier that bottled up the blaze that would have spread through the suite.

A choked sound left Nikolai. Mae's head whipped around.

Fear squeezed her heart.

He was bent over, his features distorted in pain. A haze blossomed around him. Hellfire sparked into life on Alastair's body. The crow's wings burst into flames with a whoosh.

Violet and Miles cursed and jumped out of the way. Their familiars' eyes flashed with magic.

"*Contain!*" the two of them barked at the same time as Mae repeated her spell.

Their magic wrapped Nikolai and Alastair in a layered cage.

"Brim, what's going on?!" Mae said, her voice trembling with trepidation.

The fox's eyes radiated demonic power where he stood over her, his energy and that of Hellreaver flooding her veins and augmenting her own.

"*It seems their cores are still linked to Filomena's magic. And hers is connected to her sorcerer's.*"

Mae glanced at the chameleon where she twitched and jerked within the sphere containing her. Dread knotted her shoulders.

Something must have happened to Roman!

Nikolai fell to his knees, hands grasping his belly. He met their gazes, his own wild with horror. "I—I can't control it!"

Hellfire flared in his pupils. Mae's stomach plummeted when she felt the magic building inside him.

"Get out of here!" the sorcerer shouted, his face red and the tendons in his neck cording as he struggled to suppress his core.

Alastair shuddered on the ground beside him.

Brimstone shielded Mae with his massive frame a second before Nikolai and his familiar's new powers surged from within them and blasted through the three *Contain* spells, shattering them.

Vlad cursed, his incubus energy wrapping him and Tarang in a scarlet veneer that protected them from the flames. Violet and Miles scowled where they stood behind the magic shields screening them and their familiars from the Hellfire filling the suite.

The smoke alarm came to life. Sprinklers opened in the ceiling and soaked them with a fine spray of water.

Ilya and Milo burst through the door.

Vlad cursed. "Stay back!"

The bodyguards froze in the face of the blaze rushing toward them.

"*Shield!*" Mae shouted.

Her magic rose before the two men. Hellfire crashed into the crimson wall. It held.

Mae's heart slammed against her ribs as she focused her attention on Nikolai once more, heedless of the flames warming her flesh.

Thank God for Azazel's blood!

"We need to break whatever is linking him and Alastair to Filomena!" Brimstone growled. *"It's the only way they'll be able to make that Hellfire Magic their own!"*

Mae nodded shakily, blood thundering in her ears.

A crack appeared in Miles's shield. Violet cursed as a strand of Hellfire pierced her barrier and danced near her face.

Mae closed the distance to Nikolai, dropped down before him, and shut her eyes. She took a shallow breath and focused inward, looking for the repertoire of magic hidden deep within her subconscious.

For a moment, all she saw was darkness.

A rune flickered faintly in the inky pool after what felt like a lifetime. It was followed by another.

They gained in brightness as more joined them.

Nikolai screamed in pain. The sound had Mae digging her nails into her palms.

Faster!

Hellreaver quivered against her chest as she drew on their bond. Brimstone pressed his leg against her flank, the fox lending her his power.

She grasped the runes as they finally emerged from the depths of her awareness, melded them into a conjuration, and opened her eyes.

Nikolai's hair and clothes fluttered wildly amidst the flames engulfing him. He blinked at her, barely holding on to his consciousness.

She pressed her hand to his belly and invoked the spell. *"Sever!"*

Nikolai gasped. Alastair squawked weakly.

Mae felt a bright cord snap within them.

The Hellfire brimming from their souls abated as they regained control over their cores. Nikolai swallowed convulsively and fisted his hands where he'd braced them on the floor. Brightness replaced the crimson flames in his pupils.

Mae sucked in air as Moon Magic and white magic washed across the suite, extinguishing the inferno roaring around them in a flash.

"*Mae*," Brimstone warned.

Mae looked over to where the fox stared.

It wasn't over yet.

She rose, retracted the spell containing Filomena, and lifted the convulsing chameleon in her hand. Her magic touched the corruption bubbling within the creature's core. Mae scowled.

It reeked of familiarity.

"*Barquiel!*" Brimstone snarled.

Mae gritted her teeth, drew on the power blazing inside her, and conjured another spell. "*Negate!*"

The demonic energy twisting Filomena's insides fizzled out.

The chameleon went limp in her grasp.

CHAPTER TWENTY-ONE

Roman came to slowly. He swallowed a groan, his mouth tasting like ash and his entire body aching as if he'd been pummeled by a dozen adversaries.

Muffled voices reached him as his ribcage rose and fell with deep, shuddering breaths. He kept his eyes closed and bit the inside of his cheek to stop a moan from leaving him.

The sharp cramps shooting through his muscles reminded him of what had happened, as did the echo of the corruption still throbbing in his veins from where it had filled his core and flooded his bloodstream.

The voices grew closer. A door slammed open.

"What the hell happened?!" someone barked as they stormed inside the chamber.

Roman's fingers twitched. He'd recognize that voice anywhere.

"Well?" Oscar Beneventi ground out somewhere to his right.

His lynx's hiss followed.

"The kid said something to the demon and pissed him off." The second voice belonged to the man called Dietrich. He sounded resigned. *"Rose* decided to play with him."

"Shit! That damn demon!" Oscar cursed. "I go away for ten minutes to take a piss and have a drink and that bastard waltzes in from God knows where and decides to ruin my fucking plans! Where is he anyway?!"

"I don't know. He was mumbling something about Mae when he came out of the room."

Roman felt tension coil through the air around him.

"Mae?" Oscar repeated in a deadly tone.

"Yeah."

Who's Mae?

Footsteps approached the table he lay upon. It took all of Roman's willpower not to flinch when he felt Oscar's hand brush his belly.

The sorcerer blew out a sigh. "Good. She didn't damage his core."

"Any news on the location of his familiar?" Dietrich said.

"Not yet. I'm still not sure what the hell he did that made her disappear."

Relief flooded Roman. *Thank God! Filo is still safe!*

Oscar's next words sent ice skittering down his spine.

"The most likely place she might end up is the Council of the Moon."

"Isn't that where your brother is rumored to be?" Dietrich asked curiously.

Oscar's voice shook with rage. "That bastard isn't my brother!"

"Alright, alright," Dietrich said soothingly. "Half-brother then."

"The son of a bitch must be having a whale of a time with his new family," Oscar sneered. "Maybe I should pay them a visit. Rough them up a bit, like I did his whore of a mother."

A stilted pause followed.

"Didn't you kill his mother?" Dietrich said.

Roman practically felt Oscar smile.

The sorcerer chortled. "The look on his face when she died in his arms was priceless."

Roman masked a scowl. *This monster!*

"Shame you lost the spies you'd planted in the Council of the Moon," Dietrich mused.

Oscar's tone darkened. "There are other ways we can find the information we want. Is Raya in her chambers?"

"She's having a video call with your father."

"Good."

Though he had his eyes closed, Roman could tell Oscar was staring at him. He could feel the sorcerer's gaze boring into his face like a foul sun.

"Fix the kid up and take him back to his cell." Oscar turned and headed toward the exit. "The minute we find his familiar, his core is mine. I think he's the key that will finally give us access to Hellfire Magic."

Dread sent bile surging to the back of Roman's throat.

I have to get out of here!

The face of the woman he'd seen fleetingly during the minutes he'd passed out flashed before his inner vision. He'd thought he'd dreamt her up. The more he thought about it, the more he felt convinced he hadn't.

Because he'd felt her magic through his bond with Filomena just as he'd likely visualized her through his familiar's eyes. And it was her incredible power that had shattered the demon's hold on his core.

I need to find her. But how?!

❄

"My aunt specializes in Arcane Magic," Cortes said.

"Arcane Magic?" Budimir repeated.

With Vlad's quarters out of action, they were having breakfast in Cortes's suite. Budimir had just joined them.

Cortes dipped his chin. "It's primordial magic passed down through the generations in our family." He paused and glanced at Brimstone. "I suspect one of my ancestors learned it directly from Azazel himself."

"What does Arcane Magic do?" Nikolai asked Cortes curiously.

The Colombian's expression grew awkward. "It gives someone the ability to bend the elements to their will. In rare cases, they can...see through time, bend space, and create illusions."

"Bend space?" Violet said, shocked.

Cortes nodded. "Warp it, basically."

Mae's pulse quickened at that. *I wonder if that's one of*

the reasons it's so hard to pin down the location of the Dark Council when they're close by!

She already knew from her clash with Oscar and Barquiel in Philadelphia that one of the ways the demon helped conceal dark magic users from her *Nullify* spell was by creating a portal to Hell her magic could not penetrate around them.

It might be, Brimstone said. *Time warping is advanced magic.*

"There are certain herbs Raya has to consume to feed her core and enable her to use her powers," Cortes continued. "It's not exactly the kind of stuff you find in a drugstore. I have my men searching the city for places that sell them."

Vlad frowned. "There's a chance she's still in Budapest."

Nikolai shook his head, his face grim. "She's in Prague. One of my contacts messaged me this morning. She was seen leaving Budapest with Oscar, Dietrich, and—" he paused and glanced at Mae, "Rose, a few days ago."

Mae clenched her jaw at the mention of her best friend's name. She suspected the demon possessing her knew she was in Prague too, after last night's debacle. She'd felt Barquiel's rage when she'd put an end to whatever torture he had been putting Roman through.

She hadn't told Budimir the details of what she'd sensed through Filomena's core. There was no point tormenting the guy more than he was already suffering.

"The local gangs working for the Bratva are looking

into strange deaths that may have happened in the capital these past couple of months," Budimir said. "They're also canvassing the streets to find out if there have been any unusual sightings of a group we don't know about." The old man faltered as he met their gazes, his own face dark. "I don't know if it will be of any help to you."

Mae could tell he was frustrated at his helplessness in the face of a foe he had never encountered before. "Right now, even the smallest clue would be of use."

Budimir looked grateful at her words. His gaze shifted to Filomena where the chameleon was clinging to Nikolai's chest.

The sorcerer had used his Moon Magic to soothe her strained core last night and this morning. The familiar seemed to have formed an attachment to him as a result. Alastair looked like he had mixed feelings about this. He perched on Nikolai's shoulder, his beady eyes examining the chameleon intently, like she was about to snatch his sorcerer away at any moment.

Nikolai's cellphone chirped. He looked at the screen and took the call. "Hi, Marlena." His face relaxed. "Yeah, I'm okay. No, our cores are fine. Mae checked us over this morning."

Mae found herself the focus of Vlad's stare.

"He stayed the night?" the incubus said in clipped tones.

CHAPTER TWENTY-TWO

"He slept on the couch," Mae said defensively.

Vlad lowered his brows. "Why couldn't he have stayed in Miles's room?"

Mae lifted her chin. "Because I wanted to keep an eye on his and Alastair's cores."

"Is this a lover's spat?" Budimir asked Cortes in a low voice.

"It seems so," the Colombian replied. "You could have cut the sexual tension with a knife when we were flying over here." He shrugged at Mae and Vlad's expressions. "What? It's the truth."

Budimir turned to Violet. "I thought she had a thing going with him."

He indicated Nikolai.

"She has a thing going with both of them," the witch said wryly. "They're equal contenders for the position of the Witch Queen's consort."

"Is there a rule that says she can't have both of them?" Cortes asked curiously.

"You guys know I can hear you, right?" Mae told Cortes and Violet coolly.

Hellreaver snickered.

"Is her weapon laughing at her?" Budimir said dully.

Miles grimaced. "They have a complex relationship."

Mae noted Nikolai going suddenly still.

"What?!" the sorcerer said stiffly into his cell.

Unease fluttered through her at his frown.

A muscle twitched in Nikolai's jawline. "When?" He swore as he listened to Marlena's reply. "Okay, thanks for the heads-up. I'll let them know you want to meet with them when they turn up."

He ended the call and looked up into a barrage of stares.

"A delegation from the main Vissarion house landed in Prague an hour ago. They're on their way here."

Vlad's eyes flashed crimson. Tarang growled.

Budimir's brows lowered in a thunderous scowl. "That damn hag is in Prague?!"

A disturbance outside Cortes's suite drew their gazes to the door.

Incubus power detonated around Vlad. Tarang's hackles rose.

"Looks like she's already here," Budimir said bitterly.

Mae jumped to her feet when she felt a burst of magic coming from the corridor. One of Cortes's bodyguards cried out. A gunshot shattered the air. Ilya cursed.

The door smashed under Milo's weight as he came crashing through it.

Mae's eyes rounded.

"*Levitate!*" she barked.

A scarlet bubble formed around the bodyguard, halting him inches before he collided head-first with a sideboard. His clothes were scorched over his chest from where a spell had knocked him out.

Vlad and Nikolai rushed over to the unconscious man while Mae carefully lowered him to the ground. Nikolai unleashed his Moon Magic and pressed his hands to Milo's wound. Vlad watched on with a mixture of concern and anger.

Mae switched her attention to the door.

Ilya, Cortes's men, and Budimir's guards were backing into the suite, weapons aimed squarely at the six dark-clad figures who followed them inside. She studied the Fire Magic brimming in the strangers' eyes and hands with a scowl.

"Stand down," Budimir told his men coldly. "Bullets won't work on these bastards."

Cortes dipped his chin stiffly at his escort.

The guards lowered their guns. Ilya faltered before dropping his hand to his side, his jaw clenched tight.

An elderly woman with ash-white hair raised in a bun, an impatient expression, and an ivory cane stormed past the Fire Magic users. Her rheumy eyes narrowed when she spotted Budimir.

"Where is he? Where is my great-grandson?!"

Her voice rose stridently, the red salamander on her shoulder tasting the air with its tongue.

Budimir rose, practically spitting with rage.

The woman registered Vlad's presence where he crouched by Milo. Her lip curled. "What are you doing here, *mongrel?*"

Mae's gut twisted. *Shit. Is that Vlad's grandmother?!*

She possesses strong Fire Magic, Hellreaver grumbled where he hovered defensively in front of her, his blades glinting with a hint of crimson.

I agree, Brimstone grunted beside her. *She must be the head of the Vissarion family.*

Mae could not deny their words. She could sense the power within the old woman's core.

The diamond studs in Vlad's earlobes dropped into his hands and transformed into black swords brimming with a red haze of incubus energy. He rose and marched toward the sorcerers and witches who had attacked Milo.

"Wait!" Mae said hastily. "Let's just...let's all calm down!" She looked at the incubus's grandmother. "Tell them to put their magic away."

She jerked her head at her escort.

The Vissarion matriarch bristled. "Who are you to tell me what to do, girl?!"

Mae narrowed her eyes.

"Let me guess?" The old woman flashed a contemptuous look at Vlad. "You're one of that mongrel's escorts."

Crimson power detonated in Mae's hands.

Brimstone's hackles rose. *This damn crone!*

Unease darted across the faces of the Fire Magic

users and the old woman as they witnessed Mae's magic.

"Look, I know how you feel, but you can't hurt her," Violet warned Mae. "She's an old lady and you'll never hear the end of it from your mom and Bryony."

Vlad's grandmother recovered her composure and glowered at Violet. "Another whore of that incubus rat, I presume? Or are you servicing these despicable criminals?"

She pointed her cane at Cortes and Budimir.

Miles took a threatening step forward, his and Millie's pupils flaring gold with their magic.

"I changed my mind," Violet said in a hard voice. She glanced at Mae. "Crush her."

Vlad's grandmother sneered. "I'd like to see you try, wench!"

Her salamander's eyes flared. She tapped her cane.

Fire Magic exploded from the tip and surged across the suite toward Mae.

"*Mae!*" Vlad moved, Nikolai at his side.

Mae didn't bat an eyelid as the flames approached her. "*Devour.*"

The sphere in her right hand expanded to twice its size and swallowed the fire in a single giant gulp.

The old woman gasped.

Glass clinked and furniture rattled as Mae unleashed a violent burst of magic. The crimson wave engulfed the suite in a flash and drove nearly everyone to their knees.

Budimir and Cortes clung grimly to the table,

knuckles white as they fought the immense pressure hammering into their bodies.

Shocked cries escaped the Fire Magic users when Brimstone transformed into the nine-tailed fox. They backpedaled as he stepped forward and lowered his giant head, flecks of drool dropping on the floor at their feet where his pointed fangs glinted inches from them.

Vlad's grandmother looked past the demonic familiar to Mae, her face pale and her eyes full of grudging respect. She gripped her cane and struggled to stay upright.

"Witch Queen." A muscle jumped in her cheek as she bowed curtly. "Please excuse my blunder. I did not know who you were."

She signaled to her escort. They put their Fire Magic away.

Mae watched them for a moment longer to make sure they would stay put, sniffed, and retracted her powers. "Right, now that everyone's released some tension, how about we sit down and talk, like civilized people?"

Budimir, Cortes, and their men breathed sighs of relief at being able to move again.

A metallic chomping reached Mae.

Hellreaver was snapping his serrated teeth close to one of the ashen faces of the Fire Magic users. The sorcerer's eyes rolled back in his head as he fainted.

The weapon froze when Mae pinned him with an accusing stare.

What? he said guiltily. *I still have some pent-up tension to release.*

Brimstone made an approving noise as he shrank back down to his small fox form.

CHAPTER TWENTY-THREE

Ludmila Vissarion's knuckles whitened on her cane. "Roman was kidnapped by the Dark Council?"

Vlad lowered his brows at her distraught expression. *She looks like she actually cares about his fate rather than his potential as one of her pawns.*

Budimir wasn't convinced by the Vissarion matriarch's sincerity either.

"How did you find out about Roman?" he ground out. "I made sure to keep him hidden from your clutches all these years. Which scumbag dared betray my trust?!"

A bout of sympathy shot through Vlad at Budimir's fury. Instead of using his grandson's powerful magic for his own ends, he had done his utmost to give him a normal life and protect him from those who would abuse his abilities. It was the exact opposite of how Ludmila had treated Katarina Vissarion.

I have to admire the guy, if only for that.

From Mae's friendly bearing toward the Bratva

general, she shared Vlad's feelings on this matter. It concerned him somewhat that she'd managed to charm so many high-level criminals in a such a short time, from Yuliy to Cortes, and now Budimir. He masked a grimace.

She'll probably have the head of our Bratva eating out of her hand the minute she meets him.

"It wasn't one of your men," Ludmila said dismissively. "Let's just say the Dark Council isn't the only one who has spies in relevant places."

Nikolai tensed at that. Vlad didn't miss Mae's slight squint.

The only ones who knew about Roman were the Council of the Moon and the people in the room.

"How powerful is Roman's Fire Magic?" Ludmila asked brusquely.

Budimir's face reddened.

"Wait." Mae placed a hand on his arm before he exploded. "I don't think she means it the way you think she does." She studied Ludmila carefully. "Why do you want to know?"

"Because three members of our extended family have been attacked by the Dark Council in the past month."

Mae's pulse quickened as Ludmila's bombshell statement echoed across the suite.

"We rarely move alone, so the witch and sorcerers who were targeted were able to escape, though barely," the old woman continued bitterly. "We were investigating the reasons Oscar Beneventi and Vedran could be targeting us after all this time when I was made aware of the incident in Prague and learned of Roman." She faltered, her voice fading to a whisper. "If they have him in their clutches and he's weak, it doesn't bear thinking what his fate will be."

Budimir fisted his hands.

"What do you intend to do with Roman if we find him alive?" Mae asked quietly.

"I will help him master his Fire Magic," Ludmila replied immediately.

Vlad raised an eyebrow in disbelief. "That's all?" He leaned his elbows on the table, barely holding on to the anger storming his veins. "You expect me and Budimir to believe you're not planning on putting a chain around his neck, like you did my mother?"

He couldn't stop the resentment underscoring his words. Budimir flashed him a surprised look.

Ludmila looked like she'd aged ten years when Vlad mentioned Katarina Vissarion.

"I won't make that mistake again," she said bitterly. "It cost my daughter her life in the end."

A fraught silence ensued.

"Roman is as powerful as Katarina was," Budimir confessed gruffly. "Possibly more."

Ludmila's head snapped up. "He is?!"

Mae nodded. "Yes. Even I can attest to the strength of his magic from what I felt through his familiar's core."

She hesitated. *I don't think I should be the one telling her he can access ley lines too. That privilege belongs to Roman alone.*

Ludmila blinked. "His familiar?"

Mae indicated Filomena where she clung to Nikolai's shoulder. "Roman saved her before Oscar captured him. It's probably the reason they're both still alive."

Admiration brightened the old woman's eyes as she studied the chameleon. "He's a smart boy." She gave Budimir a reluctant look of approval. "You taught him well."

"I had little to do with his magic abilities," the Bratva general said curtly. "Eleanora gave Katarina's journal to Roman."

Ludmila paled. "A journal?"

Budimir nodded. "He's been practicing his magic in secret using her knowledge."

Ludmila seemed fairly stunned at that.

"What are they after?" the old woman finally said. Her gaze turned calculating as she looked around the table. "What do you know? I doubt this little meeting of yours was for social reasons."

Mae swallowed a sigh. *She really is demanding, isn't she?*

She summarized the events that had brought them to Prague, carefully omitting the incident from the night before. Ludmila's eyes rounded as she listened. The old woman interjected sharply with pointed questions from time to time.

"They can't be after Fire Magic users just to kill them," Ludmila muttered after a tense lull. "I can't see the point of Vedran expending energy on such a fruitless venture."

"We think they're trying to use Fire Magic users'

cores in one of their schemes." Mae paused. "The caliber of Fire Magic users they've kidnapped to date may have been too poor for them to achieve their goal, which is why they're still hunting for people who harbor that magic. But now that they have Roman in their grasp…"

A glum silence befell them.

"We need to rescue him and soon," Ludmila said in a steely voice. She gave Mae a hard look. "The Vissarions' powers are at your disposal, Witch Queen."

Mae blinked, surprised. Even Vlad and Budimir looked shocked at the old witch's proposition.

"Can you use *Reveal* to identify Roman's location?" Violet asked Mae. "I mean, his familiar is here."

Mae shook her head. "I already tried. Like I suspected, Barquiel must have erected a portal around their location." She frowned at Nikolai. "We can't risk Nikolai accessing the ley line to trace Roman's Fire Magic either. It might expand the crack in the nexus."

Ludmila recoiled. "There's a crack in the nexus?!"

Nikolai dipped his chin grimly.

"By the way, Marlena wants you to pay an official visit to the Council of the Moon," he told the old woman.

"I was planning to do that anyway," Ludmila said dismissively. "It would be rude not to pay my respects to her considering I'm in her city."

Mae and Cortes glanced at the smashed-up door of his suite.

Ludmila noted their expressions. "What?"

Mae grimaced. "Your, er, priorities are a bit contradictory."

"Yes, well, I had more important matters on my mind, what with me finding out about my precious great-grandson and all."

She and Budimir exchanged glowers.

Ludmila's sharp gaze swung to Mae and Vlad. "What do you think of him?"

She pointed her cane imperiously at Vlad.

Vlad stared.

Mae blinked. "What do you mean?"

"What are his powers like? Are you two a couple? Any thoughts about babies?" Ludmila fired out. "His incubus energy and your demonic magic make for a perfect match. Your children would be a force to be reckoned with." She sniffed regally. "And beautiful too."

Mae choked on air. Vlad's eyes grew heated as he waited expectantly for her answer. Nikolai's eyes shrank to slits.

Ludmila studied the sorcerer's scowl. "What's the matter with him?"

"Don't stir that hornet's nest," Cortes muttered.

Nikolai's cell phone rang. He grumbled something under his breath as he took the call. "Hi, Marlena." Tension tightened his face. "Where?"

CHAPTER TWENTY-FOUR

A GOTHIC CLOCKTOWER WITH A GREEN, COPPER CUPOLA rose against a clear blue sky at the end of a street in Old Town, less than a mile from their hotel. The SUVs they rode in pulled up to a police barricade outside the cathedral it crowned a moment later.

The officer manning the blockade checked the ID Nikolai showed him before letting them through.

"Marlena pulled some strings," the sorcerer explained at Mae's inquisitive look. "Budimir helped." He parked next to an entrance made of decorative metal doors rising beneath a beautiful, stone relief set atop ornate pilasters and a vaulted window. "The whole place is off limits for the next few hours. Forensics have already examined the crypt where the bodies were found. They'll wait until we've finished inspecting it before removing them."

Vlad, Ludmila, and three of her escort stepped out of the second vehicle. They'd left the other witches and sorcerers at the hotel with Budimir, Cortes, and Filomena.

"You sure you're up to this?" Mae asked Ludmila worriedly as they entered the deserted vestibule.

The Vissarion matriarch flashed a frown her way. "This is not my first dead body."

Her salamander Herbert hissed softly.

Mae sighed. "I meant the stairs to the catacombs. You're not exactly a spring chicken."

Vlad swallowed a snort. Ludmila's frown deepened.

"What if you fall and break something?" Mae said insistently. "I'll never hear the end of it from my mom."

"Vlad can always carry me," Ludmila asserted confidently.

Vlad's expression turned cold. "No, thanks. You can fall and break a leg for all I care." He sneered. "Better still, your neck."

"How about Nikolai and I help you down?" Mae said hurriedly as tension sparked the air between the incubus and his grandmother.

They navigated an enormous, triple-naved space full of marble inlays, colorful ceiling frescoes, and an impressive organ rising on a loft above the entrance. Mae's gaze danced over the multitude of side chapels with their lavish sculptures and arches, before focusing on the altar they were approaching.

An elaborate, gilded, framed painting dozens of feet high and supported by a choir of angels rose above it. Tucked to either side below were two doors.

Julius was waiting for them outside the one on the left. "This way."

It was clear from his grim look that the discovery the Council of the Moon had made beneath the church was not going to be pleasant.

"The sister of one of the clergyman who works here is a witch in our council," the sorcerer explained in a low voice as he led them down a cloister and through another door. "He could tell from the state of the bodies he discovered that their deaths had not been from natural causes. He informed her before the authorities."

A narrow, stone staircase appeared at the end of the passage they were navigating. Heavy silence blanketed them as they descended into the catacombs beneath the building, the thick walls blocking out all sounds but for their footsteps and their breathing.

A chain of pale bulbs illuminated the gloomy space they entered. It cast their shadows on the walls and low, vaulted ceiling of a wide passage with ossuaries branching off on either side.

Miles shivered. "This is a nice and cheerful way to spend an afternoon."

"It beats trying to stop Budimir and the old ha—woman from tearing each other's throat out," Violet muttered.

Ludmila looked at her sharply, her cane tapping out a beat that echoed against the stone walls.

I can sense death all around us, Brimstone said somberly.

Yeah. Hellreaver quivered against Mae's chest. *This place is giving me the heebie-jeebies.*

Mae made a face. *Sometimes, I wonder if you two really were in Hell at all.*

A musty smell wafted in the cool, underground air as they moved deeper inside the mausoleum. Mae exchanged a troubled glance with Nikolai and Vlad. It grew stronger when they approached a doorway at the end of the catacombs. Mae drew a sharp breath when they stepped through the opening and stopped on a landing.

They were standing halfway up an immense, fifty-foot-high, circular crypt whose ceiling was lost in gloom. Recesses brimming with human bones and skulls lined the walls.

The sightless eyes of the dead looked down upon the bodies lying haphazardly in the glare of several spotlights on the floor below.

Tension knotted Mae's shoulders as she studied the corpses. From the way their limbs, spines, and jaws were contorted, the men and women had died violently and painfully.

Julius frowned at the garish display. "The medical examiner thinks the cause of death is likely to be severed spines and internal bleeding. She said she'd never seen anything like it in her career."

"I'd be surprised if anyone had," Ludmila said tartly. She eyed the narrow stairs snaking down the wall to their right with a distrustful look. "I'll stay up here. You young ones can tell me what you find."

Ludmila's escort accompanied them as they descended the long flight of steps. Mae's skin prickled when they reached the bottom.

An oppressive atmosphere filled the base of the crypt.

"You feel that?" Vlad said warily.

"Yes." Mae scanned the shadows beyond the lights. "We should stay on our guard."

Alastair let out a soft squawk of apprehension from Nikolai's shoulder. Everyone's face tightened as they glanced at the tiers of grinning skulls staring at them.

Mae approached the first body. It was that of a young woman.

She looked away from her milky eyes, squatted, and placed her hand an inch above the witch's belly. She focused her magic toward where the latter's core should be.

Surprise jolted her. Though damaged, the witch's core was still intact. Mae stared at the other bodies, her pulse quickening.

Wait. Does this mean they're not Fire Magic users?!

It seems not. Brimstone sniffed the dead woman. *I cannot detect any trace of the power I sensed in Filomena.* A low growl rumbled out of his chest. *But I can smell a vestige of corruption. It was definitely black magic that killed her.*

Mae frowned. She could also feel the dark residue tainting the woman's insides. There was something else there. Something she couldn't quite make out.

What is that?

I'm not sure. Brimstone's ears pricked. *It feels like some kind of...tether?*

Violet's voice startled her. "Mae? Did you find something?"

Mae nodded jerkily. "Yes. Let me check the other bodies."

The others watched on uneasily as she examined the remaining sorcerers and witches. Mae made the same stark discovery in all of them.

"Well?" Nikolai asked as she straightened from where she'd finished inspecting the last corpse.

"None of these people was a Fire Magic user. They may be dead, but their cores are still present."

Confusion clouded the faces around her.

Vlad lowered his brows. "So, they *weren't* killed by the Dark Council?"

"No. They were." Mae frowned at the sorcerer at her feet. "Brim and I can feel black magic in their cores." She paused, a muscle jumping in her jawline. "By my estimation, these bodies are at least two months old, if not older."

Julius flinched. "What?" He glanced at the victims. "But—shouldn't they be in a more advanced stage of decomposition?!"

"The space down here is cold and airtight." Mae indicated the heavy, metal door at the top of the stairs. "Now that that's open, the decomposition process will resume."

"Does this mean these attacks preceded the ones involving Fire Magic users?" Nikolai said after a short silence, his tone hard.

"Yes." Mae fisted her hands. "It seems we were mistaken."

"About what?" Violet asked cautiously.

"About the Dark Council lying low," she replied

bitterly. "It looks like they've been working hard in the shadows to achieve some goal we weren't even aware of."

Her bleak words had everyone frowning.

Miles scratched his head. "There's something I don't get."

"What?" Violet muttered glumly.

"Where are their familiars?" The sorcerer waved a vague hand around the crypt. "Shouldn't their bodies be next to them?"

Mae blinked. *He's right!*

"What did you find?" Ludmila shouted down to them.

Mae looked up distractedly, her mind racing. "They weren't Fire Ma—!"

She froze, her eyes widening.

CHAPTER TWENTY-FIVE

Ludmila recoiled when Mae raised a hand toward her.

"*Shield!*" Mae yelled.

A crimson barrier detonated above Ludmila.

The cat who'd leapt from the wall of the crypt crashed into it with a snarl. The familiar glared at the shocked Fire Magic witch, a vile darkness oozing out of its eyes. It started shuddering violently.

Mae cursed when its body silently imploded into a dark miasma. Hell's corruption swamped the crypt as a demon with red eyes and an arrowhead-tipped tail crawled out of the black cloud.

Julius stumbled back a step. "What the—?!"

Moon Magic whooshed into life around his hands.

Herbert's pupils detonated with Fire Magic. Ludmila cast a blast at the demon.

It evaded the attack, its body blurring as it leapt straight across the vault. Its claws raked lines in the stone and rained fine dust upon the ground when it landed on the opposite wall on all fours, its stance defying gravity.

A noise dragged Mae's alarmed gaze from the fiend as it focused its attention on them.

Bones were shifting in several of the recesses around the crypt.

Her stomach dropped. More familiars emerged from behind the ancient human remains, the stench of corruption radiating off them so strong it left a taste of ash in her mouth.

"Just so we're clear, are we dealing with demon-possessed zombie pets here?" Miles said, pale-faced.

Mae and the others exchanged glances.

Vlad shrugged. "It's as good a description as any."

Incubus energy sparked around him. His and Tarang's pupils flashed crimson as his swords appeared in his hands.

"Here they come," Violet warned, her fingers tightening on her arming sword.

Magic swelled across the base of the crypt as everyone drew on their powers. Brimstone shifted into his giant form. Hellreaver detached from Mae's neck and transformed.

The demons inside the familiars converging on them emerged with silent implosions that made the air tremble and Mae's ears throb. Spell bombs filled the air as they dropped toward them.

The blasts missed most of the fiends.

"Shit!" Nikolai snarled, knuckles whitening as he spun his spear. "They're fast!"

"Move to the center of the floor!" Mae barked. "*Now!*"

They crowded together, shields falling into place around and above them and Brimstone where the fox towered over their group. The demons smashed into the barriers with vicious screeches.

The walls held.

The demons jumped back and attacked again and again.

Orbs of Fire Magic arrowed down from Ludmila's hands where she stood in a protective cage of flames at the top of the stairs. The spell bombs skimmed the fiends. The old witch cursed.

Mae's heart thundered against her ribs as she tried to follow the creatures' lightning-fast moves. "Brim, are they a new species of demon? I've never seen one move this quickly before! Or that tail!"

"They are not so much new as rare." The fox growled. *"These fiends are devils. They belong to one of Hell's highest echelons of demon-like beasts and are Barquiel's faithful followers."*

Mae gritted her teeth at the mention of the demon archduke.

One of the devils pierced a Fire Magic user's shield. The witch cried out as talons raked her arm. Violet raised a second barrier to protect her.

A fine crack arced across Miles's shield. Julius's barrier trembled.

Dammit!

Heat bloomed inside Mae's belly. She rose, her hair

fluttering around her where she levitated inside a bubble of her magic with Hellreaver and Brimstone.

"*Wind Fury!*"

A storm of inky and crimson currents exploded across the crypt. It smashed into the devils and swept half of them into the air. The remaining monsters continued attacking the layered wall protecting the group below.

It shattered seconds later.

A devil escaped *Wind Fury* and leapt toward her as firebombs and destructive spells smashed into the monsters charging toward Nikolai, Vlad, and the others. Mae lowered her shield, roundhouse kicked the creature in the gut in midair, and sliced a deep wound in its belly with Hellreaver.

The monster screeched as the weapon chomped down on its flesh.

Brimstone closed his jaws on the devil's head and bit down. Black blood spurted between his fangs as he crushed the monster's neck.

More devils broke free of *Wind Fury*. Ludmila's Fire Magic followed them as they steered clear of Mae. Bones and rock exploded around the monsters as they bolted down the walls of the crypt to join the battle on the ground. One of them screeched and fell, half its body gone.

Ludmila let out a jubilant shout.

Vlad's blades and Nikolai's spear flashed as they landed cuts on the enemy, their eyes glowing with power while Tarang and Alastair bolstered their cores.

Violet's sword and Miles's saber inflicted nicks and gashes on the monsters crowding around them.

It's not enough! Dread twisted Mae's belly. She looked up at the shadowy ceiling. *I can't use* Eclipse *in here! It might bring the whole place down on our heads!*

Brimstone finally tore the devil's head off and swallowed it whole. *"Use* Decimate."

Mae's pulse stuttered while Hellreaver consumed the rest of the devil's body with happy munching sounds. She'd never heard of that spell before.

"That sounds like it might destroy this place too!"

"No. Decimate *can isolate your enemy and get rid of them without inflicting secondary damage on your surrounding or allies."*

Mae squinted. "Why haven't I heard of this spell before?"

Brimstone spat out the devil's lower jaw. *"I'm not the witch here."*

Mae scowled. She closed her eyes and focused inward.

The spell was deeper than the others she'd uncovered to date. It rose from her subconscious as if emerging from a pool of molasses, the runes resisting her grasp when she reached for them. Frustration churned her stomach.

She could hear Vlad and Nikolai's grunts and feel their magic flickering violently beneath her.

Come on, you damn spell! Faster!

The conjuration finally formed in her mind. Mae's eyes snapped open. She raised her hands.

"Decimate!"

A black and crimson orb crackled into life inches from her fingers. Mae blinked, shocked. The lightning it contained resembled the power Barquiel wielded.

Talons scored Vlad's chest. The incubus bared his teeth and blocked the devil's next attack with both swords. Ludmila's magic crashed into the monster and took it to the ground.

Vlad spun around and glared at his grandmother. "I don't need your help, old hag!"

"Shut up, you ingrate!" Ludmila snapped.

"Jesus!" Nikolai snarled. "Can you two skip the family drama for one second and focus?!"

Mae flexed her fingers.

Deadly currents arced from *Decimate*. They snaked through the air and found the devils with unerring accuracy. The monsters screamed as her magic pierced their bodies. They writhed for breathless seconds, pinned in place by a power they could not escape.

Her breath caught as they started to disintegrate from the inside out. The devils vanished in a hazy cloud of black ash that soon coated the floor.

"Vlad!" Mae headed for the incubus and touched down close to him. "Are you okay?!"

"Not really," Vlad groaned.

He was bent over and clutching his chest.

She looked over wildly at Nikolai. "Can you heal him?!"

The sorcerer nodded grimly and crossed the floor toward them.

Vlad straightened hastily. "Wait! I don't need him!"

Mae and Nikolai stared, puzzled. A wave of incubus

charm swamped the crypt, causing several sorcerers and witches to flush.

A seductive smile curved Vlad's mouth. "A kiss from my queen is all I need to make me all better."

He gazed hotly at her and puckered his lips. She punched him in the ribs, much to Tarang's chagrin.

"Ouch."

Nikolai glared at the grinning incubus while Violet, Miles, and Julius sighed. "You deserved that, asshole."

CHAPTER TWENTY-SIX

"What did you say?"

Tension hummed through Oscar as he stared at Dietrich.

"Word on the street is that the kid is Budimir Volkov's grandson," the Immortal said warily.

Oscar lowered his brows. "As in, that Bratva general everyone is scared of?"

Dietrich dipped his chin.

Oscar twisted around and stared out of the leaded window of his temporary accommodation, his mind racing. Sunlight glinted on the still waters below.

The abandoned fortress they were using as their base stood in the middle of a lake, a lone sentry that had seen scores of battles in times past. It was only accessible by boat and the secret tunnel that ran deep underground beneath the woods surrounding it. The old man who'd lived in a cabin close to the mine concealing the entrance had been disposed of weeks ago. No one knew they were here.

A muscle jumped in Oscar's cheek. *And with Barquiel's portal around us, that damn witch can't find us either.*

The demon had finally reappeared that morning, his mood subdued. Oscar suspected he'd visited the place he always vanished to for hours on end. He'd finally questioned the demon about it a few weeks ago, when they'd still been in Budapest.

Barquiel had morphed out of Rose's body and gripped him by his neck before slamming him against the wall of Vedran's study.

"That's none of your business, runt!" the Archduke of Hell had spat in Oscar's face.

Raya had watched on nervously while a bored expression had drifted across Vedran's face.

"You mustn't taunt Barquiel, Oscar," the Sorcerer King had drawled. "There are certain…things we all want to keep private."

His eyes had glinted as he'd watched the demon.

Oscar frowned presently.

"It doesn't matter," he told Dietrich. "We'll deal with Volkov and his Bratva if we have to. Roman's Fire Magic core is more important."

It wasn't until later that he headed down to the dungeon beneath the medieval fortress with Drabek. Another sorcerer had died that morning, the result of his experiment a failure once more. Oscar couldn't see much point in carrying on with the remaining Fire Magic users at their disposal. The answer he sought lay inside Roman. He was certain of it.

The stench of human waste and sweat made him

curl his lip when he descended the stairs to the prison. He reached the bottom and made his way to Roman's cell, boots clacking on the stone floor while Drabek padded silently beside him.

The kid was sleeping on a thin pallet on the ground.

The sorcerers and witches in the neighboring cells stirred as Oscar invoked a weak, black-magic bomb and sent it floating through the iron bars of the prison.

"Boo."

The spell detonated above Roman. He woke up with a startled cry, bolted upright, and backpedaled until his body hugged the wall.

Oscar burst out laughing. Drabek grinned beside him.

"For the grandson of a mobster, you sure are chicken," he finally managed between chuckles.

Roman recovered his composure and glared at him. "What the hell do you mean by that?!"

Oscar wiped his eyes, full of mirth still. "There's no use being stubborn, kid. We know who your grandfather is. If you'd told us who you were in the first place, we might have treated you a little better than these rats."

He sneered at the figures cowering in the adjacent prisons.

Roman rose and approached the door, his face dark with anger. "How about you stop talking in riddles and tell me what this is about, asshole?!"

Oscar's eyes widened a little.

"I have to hand it to you, kid," he said after a pause.

"You have guts. And I mean your grandfather being a Bratva general."

Roman flinched. "Stop with your lies. My grandfather works for a benevolent organiza—!"

Oscar's laughter drowned out the rest of his words. He doubled over and wheezed, tears streaming down his face at the truth that had dawned on him. A voice had him looking around.

"What are you doing?" Rose said curiously as she came down the passage.

"Nothing much." Oscar snorted. "This kid here didn't know who his grandfather is."

A frowned darkened Rose's face. "Dietrich just told me." The demon glanced coldly at the ashen boy standing forlornly behind the bars. "You sure this won't be a problem? The Dark Council works with a lot of criminal organizations."

"Come now," Oscar drawled. "Once we get our hands on Hellfire Magic and unlock the *Book of Shadows*, not a single crime syndicate will be able to stand up to us." He manifested another sphere of black magic and sneered. "Besides, I am more than powerful enough to crush any Bratva."

Crimson gleamed in the demon's eyes. A smirk lit Rose's face. "I came here to tell you the decoy worked."

Oscar stiffened. "You mean, the trap we laid with those bodies?"

Barquiel nodded, Rose's smile radiating satisfaction. "Even though it took trial and error to figure out we needed to use the cores of Fire Magic users to access Hellfire Magic, those experiments were still worthwhile. I just felt one of the snares activate." The smile turned savage. "Considering my devils are dead, I bet Mae was the one who triggered it."

Oscar's mouth stretched in a matching grin. Drabek growled.

They left, leaving the shocked boy whose world they had just turned upside down still standing motionless inside his cell.

※

"It's been a while," Marlena told Ludmila.

The old witch grimaced. "I'm afraid events got the better of me. I would have visited sooner otherwise."

"Tell all the covens in Europe to look for traces of black magic in desolate places," Mae said in a hard voice. "Cemeteries. Mausoleums. Anywhere close to where magic users have gone missing under strange circumstances." She clenched her jaw. "But tell them not to disturb any bodies they find."

Marlena looked at her worriedly. Her terrier woofed, similarly anxious.

They'd reconvened at the Council of the Moon to get their wounds treated. Ludmila and her escort had accompanied them.

"Are you saying that those bodies were bait?" the Vissarion matriarch said sharply from where Klara was tending to her.

"Yes." Mae ran a hand through her hair. "Brim and I felt something strange inside the corpses. It looks like my magic triggered their dead familiars and activated whatever sorcery was used to turn their cores into portals for Barquiel's devils."

"That's—" Julius's voice trailed into silence.

"—some pretty sick shit," Violet mumbled.

"He must know what happened by now." Vlad thanked the witches and sorcerer who'd tended to him and shrugged into a shirt he'd borrowed off Nikolai. "If those devils are linked to him in any way, the Dark Council knows you're in Prague."

I agree, Brimstone huffed.

Miles got off the phone with Bryony. "She's going to contact the High Council and spread the word about those booby traps."

A fraught hush befell them. It was Nikolai who broke it.

"Using magic users as bait and weaponizing their familiars is a step above anything they've tried before," the sorcerer said somberly. "Their methods are getting more and more cruel."

"They have a lot at stake," Mae muttered. "Getting their hands on the soul of the first Sorcerer King has got to be their top priority right now."

Vlad's phone buzzed with an incoming text. His eyes flared. "It's Cortes." He looked up and met Mae's questioning gaze, his own bright with excitement. "He has a lead on Raya Medeiros."

CHAPTER TWENTY-SEVEN

A TOWN CAR WITH A PRIVATE NUMBER PLATE PULLED UP outside a shabby store with graffiti-covered walls in Zizkov, in Prague's third district. A woman in a long, black, hooded cloak stepped out of the vehicle, cast a furtive look around, and headed inside.

"That's her," Nikolai said in a hard voice.

Cortes's knuckles whitened. He leaned past the driver's seat.

"You sure this was a good idea?" Vlad murmured to Mae as they watched an expression of pure loathing darken the Colombian's face where he sat between them in the back of the SUV.

"The guy didn't leave us much of a choice." Mae grimaced. "At least we managed to persuade Budimir and Ludmila to wait at the hotel."

The Bratva general and the Vissarion matriarch had protested vehemently when Mae had decided on the group who would accompany them to trail Raya.

"Look," Mae had finally said, frustrated. "I'm afraid

you'll do something that will jeopardize this whole mission and get yourselves hurt. You are far too emotional right now." She'd glowered at Budimir. "And *you*, old guy, have no magic, so don't even think about following us. The last thing Roman needs after we rescue him is to find out his grandfather died because of his own folly!"

Budimir's eyes had shrunk to slits at that. "I can still fight."

"Not if I destroy your weapons," Mae had retorted.

"You wouldn't dare!"

Mae had curled a lip. "Watch me."

"She's right," Ludmila had said stiffly. "We'll only get in the way of the young ones." The old witch had fixed Mae with a piercing look. "But you're taking my escort."

"Don't you need at least one of them to stay behind and feed you your embalming pills?" Vlad had sneered.

Mae had sighed as the incubus and his grandmother had launched into a heated verbal tirade. She'd taken one look at Cortes's face and decided that battle wasn't worth fighting.

Besides, I would want to be around too if someone tracked down the person who hurt Brimstone and cracked my core.

"Here she comes," Julius muttered where he sat beside Nikolai.

Raya exited the shop with a small brown bag in her hand and got inside the town car. It pulled away from the curb seconds later.

Nikolai drove out of the spot where he'd parked

and followed at a safe distance, the vehicle carrying Violet, Miles, and three Fire Magic users on their tail. A contingent of sorcerers and witches from the Council of the Moon was tracking them in a van, their GPS locked on Nikolai's cell.

They drove some twelve miles north of Prague and soon entered a densely forested area. The town car slipped in and out of view between the trees ahead of them as it headed up a tortuous mountain road, the dying sunlight piercing the canopy to glint off its taillights.

"Shit." Nikolai's hands tightened on the steering wheel after they rounded a turn. "Where'd it go?"

He slowed to a crawl. The way ahead was empty.

Cortes was staring out the rear windshield. "There are tire tracks thirty feet behind us."

Mae followed his gaze and peered into the gathering gloom. "Where?"

"Trust me, they're there."

Nikolai reversed just as Violet's vehicle caught up with them.

Vlad pointed out his window. "He's right."

Mae stared. The vegetation was rolling back to cover a faint trail.

She gave Cortes a look of admiration. "You have eyes like a hawk. Maybe we should get you a bird familiar if I manage to fix your core."

Cortes arched an eyebrow. "The familiar normally chooses their magic user."

Mae looked at Brimstone. "They do?"

The fox huffed in agreement.

Julius called the team in the van and told them where to turn off the road. Undergrowth snapped and rustled around them as they headed into the darkening forest.

Nikolai kept the headlights off.

The shadowy outcrop of a hill loomed out of the trees to their right a mile later. They passed an abandoned cabin and soon pulled up on the edge of a lake.

Julius stared out over the dark waters. "There's nothing here."

Vlad scanned the inky gloom. "Where's the town car?"

Mae blinked. She'd just sensed something. Something faint, but dark and insidious, nonetheless. Brimstone's hackles rose.

There's a portal to Hell close by, he growled.

Nikolai startled when Mae opened the passenger door and jumped out with the fox. "Where are you going?"

"There's something here."

Mae walked to the water's edge. The others joined her as she squatted on the shoreline. Crimson magic flared at her fingertips. She dipped her hand in the shallows, concentrated her power into a faint, thin line, and aimed it at where she'd felt the anomaly.

Weak ripples broke out as the magic thread danced beneath the surface of the lake. It arrowed straight and true toward the center of the body of water, only to vanish after some four hundred feet.

Power surged through Mae. "*Reveal.*"

The air trembled with a violent, red haze for scant seconds. Shadowy ramparts and towers with lit windows shimmered dimly into view before disappearing behind the invisible rift that had shielded them from sight.

"What the hell?!" Julius mumbled.

"Hell is exactly what we just looked through," Mae said bitterly.

"Was that a castle?" Violet asked.

She and Miles had joined them.

"It sure looked like it," Vlad said grimly.

"I can't see any boats." Cortes was looking around with a frown. "There must be a tunnel somewhere close by."

They returned to their vehicles and did a U-turn. The cabin appeared between the trees. They stopped outside it.

The place looked like it had been lived in recently. Julius found clothes belonging to a man in a closet and blood pressure tablets in the cabinet in the bathroom.

It was Brimstone who sniffed out the body buried in a shallow grave behind the ramshackle building. Anger stirred inside Mae as she studied the decomposing corpse of the elderly man they'd dug up. His neck had been snapped.

She crouched and scanned his remains with her powers. "I can sense a faint trace of the Dark Council's magic."

"And I can smell engine oil," Cortes said.

He was staring at the hill blocking out the lower half of the sky to the west.

Mae squinted. *This guy really does have the instincts of a beast.*

Indeed, Brimstone murmured. *He would make a great demon general.*

They headed over on foot and were soon joined by the Council of the Moon's sorcerers and witches who'd followed them in the van. An abandoned mine appeared at the foot of a cliff. Rotting planks covered the entrance.

"It's a dead end," Julius said, disappointed.

Cortes dropped on his haunches and traced a finger in the dirt. He brought it to his nose. "A car's been through here."

Mae stared at the barricade. "Brim?"

The fox's ears pricked forward. He scented the air. *I smell...ancient magic.*

Understanding dawned. She conjured up a crimson sphere, walked up to the wooden blockade, and punched through it.

"Mae!" Nikolai gasped. "What are you—?!"

His eyes widened as the makeshift barrier vanished under the effect of her magic.

"It's an illusion." Mae frowned at the gaping tunnel she'd uncovered. "Probably Raya's."

She felt Cortes's gaze on her as she headed into the dark void.

The mine shaft spiraled as it dropped. They came across old, rusted-metal tracks screwed into the floor and passed side passages blocked by rockfall. It appeared to have been a prolific quarry at one time.

They emerged into what looked like an old resting

area a while later. The empty town car was parked in the middle.

Cortes pressed a hand to the hood. "Engine's still warm. They can't be far."

Nikolai was about to lead the way into the tunnel beyond when Mae froze and clutched his arm. She looked around wildly, her heartbeat accelerating.

Vlad tensed. "What's wrong?"

"Brim's gone!"

I'm right here.

Mae whirled around. Her eyes bulged.

The fox's head was poking out of the solid rock some twelve feet to her right.

"That's a space warp," Cortes said grimly while everyone stared glassily.

Mae shuddered and pressed a hand to her chest before scowling at the familiar. "Don't scare me like that!"

It's not exactly my fault, Brimstone grumbled. *I thought I felt something, poked at it with my demon powers, and fell right into the damn thing.*

The fox hopped out of the concealed entrance.

Mae's skin prickled with unease. Now that she knew what to look for, she felt the magic Brimstone had detected.

"Your aunt is one hell of a witch," she muttered to Cortes.

The Colombian frowned. "I know."

"What's down there, Brim?" Mae said.

Stairs that lead to a tunnel. I think we're beneath the lower edge of Barquiel's portal.

CHAPTER TWENTY-EIGHT

"Don't do it, Roman!" The sorcerer's pupils were wide with fear behind the iron bars of his cell. "They'll kill you and probably the rest of us if they find out!"

"I have to try." Roman clenched his jaw and met the man's fearful gaze. "We're all going to die down here anyway," he said bitterly. "Might as well mess with their plans and go out with a bang."

The sorcerer went limp at that, the fight draining out of him.

Roman knelt on the floor of his cell. He frowned. *Besides, I have questions for my grandfather.*

He knew Oscar hadn't lied when he'd told him about Budimir. He'd seen the truth in the sorcerer's eyes.

There's no reason for him to deceive me. And it all makes sense now. The death threats Grandfather received. The bodyguards. I was a mafia prince and I didn't even know it!

Bitterness churned Roman's stomach. He suppressed his anger.

Raging at the world wasn't going to help him get out of this mess. The only one who could help him right now was himself. The face of the woman he'd seen through Filomena's eyes flitted before him at that thought.

I hope I live long enough to meet her and thank her for saving me and Filo that night.

Roman took a deep breath, pressed his hands to the cool stone, and reached for his magic. For a moment, all he sensed was darkness.

A flame flickered into life deep within him.

Sweat beaded his forehead as the fire grew, stinging his bruised core where Barquiel had attacked him. He invoked what strength he could muster without his familiar and blasted his power into the rock, seeking a ley line.

His magic smashed into something seconds later.

Roman was thrown clear across the cell by the explosive force of the impact. He slammed shoulder first into the metal grille and cried out as the corruption coating it burned his flesh.

The walls and floor of his prison started to tremble. A fine layer of dust rained down on him from the shuddering ceiling as he staggered backward to the middle of the cell.

"What did you do?!" the sorcerer shouted from across the way.

"I—I don't know!" Roman met his panicked stare. "That wasn't meant to happen!"

One of the witches yelped.

Roman's eyes rounded as a thin flow of water

stained the corridor outside his prison. It doubled in size.

Cold drops landed on the back of his neck, startling him. He looked up and swallowed convulsively when he spotted the fresh crack in the ceiling. It expanded even as he watched, letting in a gush of water. He jumped out of the way as the deluge crashed down.

Screams tore through the prison as dark currents rushed inside the underground dungeon. Fear twisted Roman's insides.

What—what have I done?!

Fire flared in the passage. The trapped sorcerers and witches were trying to break their way out of their cells despite the black magic burning their hands. Alas, their attempts were too weak to overcome their enemy's tremendous power.

Water swirled around Roman's thighs, jolting him out of his shocked daze. He scowled and drew on his magic. He might be weaker without Filomena but he was still strong enough to fight. He gripped the bars of his cell.

Pain scorched his palms. Roman gritted his teeth. The iron trembled in his grasp. The metal shifted to orange then a fierce red as he attempted to soften and bend it.

Air escaped him in a harsh gasp a moment later. He blinked perspiration out of his eyes. Despair choked his throat when he examined his handiwork. He'd managed to separate the bars by an inch.

The gap was still far too narrow for him to get through.

Roman's shoulders sagged. He shuddered and closed his eyes as the water rose to his chest. The torches in the corridor fizzled out, filling the air with smoke and terrified cries.

Is this how we die? In this hellhole where no one will find us?!

His grandfather's face flickered across his inner vision. Determination tightened his muscles.

No! I can't die! I still need to give that old man a piece of my mind!

Roman took several deep inhales and exhales as the icy water gurgled around his neck. He went under, grasped the iron bars, and focused his magic on the metal.

It was nearly two minutes before he felt himself struggling for breath. He kicked up, found an air pocket in the ceiling, and exhaled and inhaled harshly before swimming down to the prison door once more. Something drew his gaze in the passage outside.

A faint, crimson light. It grew in intensity.

A shocked gurgle escaped Roman when a giant fox with nine tails came into view inside an immense bubble of red magic that almost filled the corridor.

Riding him was the woman he'd seen through Filomena.

Her pupils glowed scarlet, as did the orb blazing in her hand. Though her eyes resembled Barquiel's in that moment, Roman did not fear her.

She signaled to him.

Roman nodded and kicked back to the opposite end of his cell.

Power brightened the woman's pupils. A crimson aura detonated around her, causing the bubble to tremble and casting violent eddies in the water. The orb in her hand grew incandescent.

His heart stuttered as her spell bomb sailed through the sphere and shattered his prison door in a single strike. The woman touched the medallion against her chest and watched the mangled bars drift slowly down to the floor.

Roman's eyes rounded when the pendant transformed into a vicious-looking, double-ended dagger. The weapon zoomed out of the bubble and headed to the cell opposite his. It sliced effortlessly through the metal grille, its blades glimmering red with power.

He glimpsed more shadowy figures inside crimson globes coming to rescue the other Fire Magic sorcerers and witches as he swam out of his cell. The witch reached out of the protective barrier, grabbed his wrist, and pulled him through.

Roman found himself levitating in the air pocket within the bubble. He gasped, water dripping off him and pooling at the base of the sphere.

"Are—are you Mae?!" he mumbled, unable to take his eyes off the woman in front of him.

She bobbed her head.

"Let's save the chitchat for later," she said briskly. "We have more important matters to deal with right now. Oscar and Barquiel will soon be headed this way."

Fear tightened Roman's chest.

Mae's face softened when she saw the wounds on

his hands and his shoulder. "We'll take care of those later too."

She guided the bubble out of the flooded prison and up the stairs. Her allies followed, the Fire Magic users they'd rescued safe within their own spheres.

A faint glow appeared above them when they emerged into the main dungeon area. They started to ascend.

Mae and the fox stiffened a moment later, their gazes swinging in tandem to stare to their left. Roman followed their lead and peered into the murky currents. His eyes rounded.

Barquiel was coming for them.

Horror filled Roman as he beheld the demon's true appearance.

CHAPTER TWENTY-NINE

A BOLT OF BLACK LIGHTNING LEFT THE WINGED monster's giant sword. It zipped through the water and smashed into the red bubble. A second and a third bolt followed rapidly.

A faint crack appeared in the crimson barrier.

Water started dripping through it.

"Shit!" Mae cursed. "Looks like we need to get out of this shield to fight him!"

Roman startled when the fox spoke.

"What about the kid?" the beast rumbled.

Mae lowered her brows at Roman.

Confusion swamped him when she cast a crimson air helmet around his head. "What—what are you doing?!"

"Try not to die."

She pressed a hand to his chest and blasted him out of the sphere a second before it disintegrated.

Roman choked as he whooshed rapidly backward

through the water, Mae and the fox's figures shrinking in the distance.

Detonations boomed in his ears. He looked around wildly and saw Mae's friends engage the Dark Council sorcerers and witches attacking them from within their own black-magic bubbles. His pulse stuttered.

Several of the people fighting on Mae's side were Fire Magic users. Powerful ones at that.

Roman fisted his hands where he floated, feeling weak and helpless at not being able to aid them. A disturbance above him drew his gaze. His eyes widened.

A dark orb was arrowing down toward him. It was Oscar's.

The sorcerer looked pissed enough to kill him from where he levitated inside a corrupt sphere with his lynx familiar.

Roman tried to swim out of the path of the attack.

It followed his movements.

The orb was five feet from striking him when someone blocked it.

Shock jolted Roman as he stared at the figure with the spear and the crow glaring at Oscar from within one of Mae's red spheres. A bright light blazed from their eyes and hummed around them.

That's—that's white magic! Like in the ley lines!

Another figure appeared, two black swords in hand and a tiger with dazzling scarlet pupils at his side. Roman swallowed at the red energy shimmering around the blond man and his familiar.

It was magic unlike any he'd ever felt before.

No! It—it kinda resembles Mae's!

A fierce battle started between Oscar and the two men.

The resulting eddies swept Roman farther away. He startled and started swimming for the distant surface, steering clear of the warring sorcerers and witches around him.

A slipstream caught him when he was halfway to the top.

Panic choked Roman as the current tugged him toward the darkness at the bottom of the dungeon. He struggled valiantly, the muscles in his arms and legs burning as he fought the undertow. His vision swam.

He was running out of oxygen.

Roman's labored breathing echoed the drumming of blood in his ears as he sank to the bottom of the cave. His body touched the ground moments later. Inky spots bloomed across his sight as he slowly settled on his back. His chest grew impossibly tight.

He lifted a hand weakly toward the blurry shapes far above him.

Don't…leave me…here…

His oxygen ran out. Shudders shook him as he started to asphyxiate, the red bubble around his head the only thing stopping him from drowning as well. His eyelids fluttered closed.

Fangs gently scraped his neck. Something picked him up by the neckline of his shirt and dragged him from the bottom of the abyss. A warm hand grasped his wrist seconds later. He was tugged into someone's hold.

Fingers pinched his nose. Then a mouth covered his and blew air into his starving lungs at the same time that the bubble around his head vanished.

Roman's fading consciousness flared to life. So did his magic.

He blinked and stared into the crimson pupils of the witch who'd saved him. His core trembled. Throbbed. Swelled.

Mae was replenishing the source of power deep within him.

Ho—how?!

She lifted her lips from his, clutched his hand, and grabbed the flank of her fox familiar. Roman grasped her fingers tightly as the animal picked up pace and rose, powerful legs creating violent currents in their wake with each kick.

They emerged from the water moments later.

Roman was hauled onto a rock shelf, coughing and spluttering. He shuddered, arms and legs trembling as he struggled to stay on his hands and knees.

"You okay, kid?" Mae panted.

She was leaning on her elbows beside him.

"It's Roman."

She blinked at his low mumble.

"My name. It's Roman."

His heart skipped a beat at Mae's amused smile.

"I know," she drawled, oblivious to the hot feeling surging through him. "You have a very impatient and worried grandfather and great-grandmother waiting for your return."

Roman blinked. "Great-grandmother?!"

Mae grimaced and rose to her feet. "It's a long story."

A man hurried over to them from where he'd been waiting, the flashlight in his hand casting eldritch shadows on the walls of the freshly formed underground lake.

"Our way out is blocked," he said grimly.

He glanced at Roman before shining the bright beam back the way he'd come. A fresh rockfall appeared in the pale radiance a few hundred feet away.

The giant fox shook out his fur and drenched them with a shower just as the crimson bubbles carrying Mae's companions and the Fire Magic prisoners they'd saved bobbed to the surface of the water. The sorcerer with white magic and the red-eyed man with the tiger were with them. They started swimming toward the shoreline as the spheres protecting them vanished.

The fox tensed. *"Here they come."*

Roman felt a strong aura of corruption and the vile energy of the demon approaching from beneath the water. Oscar and Barquiel exploded from the lake, water dripping off the dark spheres enveloping them. Inky orbs and black lightning arrowed toward Mae's friends.

A crimson wave detonated around the witch and the fox, the familiar's nine tails vibrating with power. She raised her hands, her eyes bright with magic.

"Shield! Multiply!"

Roman's breath caught at the potent magic contained within the spell she'd invoked. The conjuration raised crimson barriers loaded with pale runes between her companions and Oscar and Barquiel's attack.

"Devour!" Mae barked.

The red sphere that exploded into life with her second conjuration expanded as it whizzed across the water and swallowed the orbs and the black lightning with gluttonous gulps.

Barquiel shrieked. Oscar cursed.

Mae sneered. *"Negate!"*

The third conjuration made the corruption shielding the sorcerer and the demon flicker into nothingness.

"Ice Fortress!" the witch growled before either could react.

Roman's breath misted in front of his face as the temperature around him rapidly plummeted. Glittering crystals formed in the air. The shards thickened before forming thick cages around Barquiel and Oscar.

The demon and the sorcerer's muffled bellows rose faintly as they dropped into the lake inside their prisons of ice. The surface of the water froze over.

Mae frowned. "There you are."

She extended a hand. The double-bladed dagger she had conjured from her pendant sliced through the ice and slammed into the witch's palm.

She narrowed her eyes at it. "And where have you been?"

The weapon took on a guilty vibe.

The fox sighed. *"Judging by the strands of meat caught in his teeth, he was probably eating something."*

The weapon squirmed under Mae's dark stare.

"Mae!" someone shouted.

Roman turned. The white-magic sorcerer with the crow and the red-eyed man with the tiger were closing in on them, the others lagging in their wake.

The sorcerer touched Mae's cheek gently, his worried gaze roaming her face. "Are you okay?"

He scowled when the red-eyed man barged past him and hugged her. Roman lowered his brows, similarly irked for some reason.

"Er, Vlad, now's not the time for this," Mae wheezed, pressing her hands against the blond man's chest.

He let her go reluctantly.

Violent tremors started shaking the walls around them.

"Shit," muttered a witch with purple hair and a white rabbit. "This whole place is going to come down on us!"

"Anyone seen Raya?" the man with the flashlight asked, a muscle jumping in his cheek.

Mae shook her head. "No. She's probably inside the fortress." She paused at his expression. "Don't worry. You'll get your chance for revenge."

The guy hesitated before nodding jerkily.

"Violet's right. This whole island is about to collapse." Mae studied the cave with a grim look. "Whatever crashed into the portal and caused the dungeon to flood created some kind of slipstream that's dragging everything into, well—" she grimaced, "Hell."

Roman flinched. Mae noted his reaction with a squint.

She looked at her weapon. "Hellreaver, you're up."

The weapon quivered.

Mae pointed an imperious finger at the wall. "What I mean is, I want you to carve us a way out of here."

The weapon's quivering intensified, as if it were protesting.

Magic flared threateningly around Mae. The weapon froze before sagging in her grasp.

The fox rolled his eyes, like this was a regular thing.

CHAPTER THIRTY

"Are you going to talk to me?" Mae asked for the tenth time.

Hellreaver grew even heavier where he hung around her neck in his medallion form. The weapon hadn't spoken to her once since they'd made their successful escape from the underground lake.

"Is he still sulking?" Nikolai said from the driver's seat.

"Yeah," Mae replied morosely.

Julius and Vlad grimaced.

He'll feel better once we feed him some meat, Brimstone reassured Mae.

The fox was curled up on her lap.

Cortes eyed the pendant guardedly. Hellreaver had demonstrated why he deserved to be her weapon when he'd sliced a path through some two hundred feet of rock like he was out for an afternoon stroll and led them safely to one of the mine shafts.

The weapon finally spoke when their hotel came into view.

I'm just a glorified can opener to you, aren't I? Hellreaver said sullenly.

Mae swallowed a sigh. "Look, it was in the heat of the moment." She brightened and patted him. "And you did great. You saved us all. Why, you're the hero of the hour!"

Hellreaver hesitated before lightening against her chest, practically vibrating with smugness.

It worries me how susceptible he is to compliments, Brimstone told Mae.

Tarang huffed.

Dawn was breaking across Prague when they parked outside the hotel. Roman stepped out of the second SUV with Violet and Miles.

Mae had been surprised when she'd seen him for the first time. His face, blond hair, tawny eyes, and his tall, toned frame closely resembled Vlad's.

It was easy to tell they were related.

Budimir and Ludmila met them in the foyer.

The Bratva general stormed across the floor and wrapped his grandson tightly in his arms, relief brightening his dull eyes. "Roman!"

Roman stiffened before hugging his grandfather back, his face crumpling.

Filomena hopped from Budimir's shoulder and landed on Roman's head. She gripped his hair like she never intended to let go.

Roman flushed as he pulled back and lifted the chameleon in his hands. "Filo! I'm glad you're safe!"

Filomena's eyes shrank to happy slits when he nuzzled her and rubbed her under the chin.

His expression cooled a little as he looked at his grandfather. "We need to talk. About a lot of things."

Guilt clouded Budimir's face. Ludmila practically hopped from cane to foot next to him, eager to be introduced.

"How about we take this upstairs?" Mae advised hastily, conscious of the curious eyes on them.

They took the elevators to Cortes's suite. To Mae's surprise, a serving cart laden with steak and miscellaneous dishes was waiting for them. Brimstone, Hellreaver, Tarang, and the other familiars headed for it.

She turned to Budimir and Ludmila. "Thank you."

Ludmila shrugged as guzzling sounds erupted and food debris started flying around the cart. "Something told me they'd be famished when they returned."

"Roman, this is Ludmila Vissarion," Budimir told his grandson reluctantly. "She's your maternal great-grandmother."

"Hello," Roman said hesitantly.

Ludmila smiled. "You're a handsome fellow."

Roman flushed. His gaze darted to Mae.

Mae gave him a puzzled look.

Ludmila noted the exchange with a raised eyebrow. Her face livened up, like she'd just realized something. The devious cackle she uttered sent a chill down Mae's spine and had Nikolai and Vlad stiffening.

❈

"The reason why I never told you about what I did for a living is because I wanted you to have nothing to do with that world," Budimir told Roman grimly.

Roman's face tightened, his hand stilling where he was stroking the chameleon clinging to his chest. He'd showered and changed before eating the breakfast Budimir and Ludmila had ordered for them.

Vlad studied the Bratva general and his grandson guardedly while he drank his coffee.

"So, wait," Mae hissed beside him. "The kid didn't know?!" She chomped on a mini macaroon.

"It looks that way."

It was clear Budimir had wanted to protect Roman the same way Yuliy had wished to shield him from a criminal life. Vlad frowned.

He should have talked to him about it once he got older though. At least I knew about the Bratva Yuliy worked for before I got involved in that underworld.

Vlad helped himself to a macaroon from Mae's plate. She gasped and clutched the rest protectively to her chest.

"You should know better than to steal her food," Violet told Vlad.

"That's one way to accidentally lose some fingers, dude," Miles murmured.

Millie hissed in agreement.

Cortes wordlessly passed Mae another plate of confectionaries. She brightened.

"I can't help but feel that he's slowly taming her, like some kind of circus monkey," Violet whispered to Miles.

Cortes flashed the cousins a smile that made them shiver.

"I wish you hadn't lied to me." A muscle twitched in Roman's cheek as he glared at his grandfather. "Do you how I felt when that—*that man* told me about you?! I felt like a fool. One who had lived his entire life surrounded by lies!"

Budimir flinched at his shrill tone.

Ludmila's quiet voice shattered the tense hush. "As much as I wish to see this old coot squirm, there is no denying that he did what he did to protect you."

Surprise shot through Vlad.

Roman narrowed his eyes at the old witch. "Look, I'm grateful to have met you, but I still don't trust the Vissarions. Not after what my grandmother told me about you lot."

Ludmila's escort exchanged irritated murmurs.

"Smart kid," Cortes said under his breath.

Ludmila's expression turned chagrined. She raised a hand to silence the Fire Magic users standing behind her.

"I won't deny my past actions." Lines wrinkled the witch's brow as she cast a sharp glance at Vlad. "But I wish you would judge me on my present deeds and my future path."

Vlad's stomach clenched. He couldn't help but feel that the Vissarion matriarch had intended those words for him too.

"Can you tell us what happened to you?" Nikolai asked.

Roman watched Ludmila for a beat longer before

reluctantly providing them with details about his kidnapping.

Mae leaned forward, her eyes sparkling with interest as he explained what he'd done to try and evade Oscar. "So, *Transmigrate* is the spell that allowed you to hide Filomena in the nexus?"

"Yes."

The color had drained from Ludmila's face. "You can access ley lines?!"

It was the first time she was hearing of this.

Roman nodded.

The old witch glowered accusingly at Mae and Nikolai. "Did you know?"

Mae shrugged. "It wasn't our place to tell you."

Nikolai's expression grew strained as he studied Roman. "How long have you and Filomena been able to tap into ley lines?"

Unease clouded Roman's face when he registered everyone's troubled look.

"Not long," he replied reluctantly. "I've only used them a handful of times, once I realized how to locate them. Katarina mentioned them in her journal."

Ludmila recoiled, stunned.

Vlad's heart slammed a quick tempo against his ribs. "She did?"

"Yes." Roman licked his lips and scanned their faces. "What are you guys not telling me?"

"Drawing on ley lines is not a normal ability," Mae explained gently. "Even I, the Witch Queen, don't possess that skill." Her gaze shifted briefly to Nikolai.

"As far as we knew, Nikolai was the only one in the world who could do so."

"Wait." Roman paled. *"You're the Witch Queen?!"*

He stared at Mae like she was a goddess descended upon the Earth.

Mae wrinkled her nose. "Yeah."

Nikolai leaned forward, his eyes shining with curiosity. "Do you experience any side effects when you access a ley line?"

Roman nodded, his brow furrowing. "Yes. It normally drains me and Filo of our strength."

Nikolai and Julius traded a cautious look.

"I'm the same," Nikolai told a shocked Roman. "Alastair and I used to suffer from debilitating weakness whenever we sought out a ley line."

He patted the crow as the latter nudged his cheek lovingly.

Roman blinked. "Used to?"

Nikolai dipped his chin. "I'm currently training with the Council of the Moon to overcome those side effects. It might benefit you and Filomena to do the same, once things settle."

Ludmila frowned. "Moon Magic and Fire Magic have little in common. I'm not sure training with the Council of the Moon will help him much."

"Oh." Mae blinked. "In that case, how about Sun Magic?"

Vlad stared. "You mean Nadia?"

Mae nodded. "There's no harm asking her for her opinion."

Vlad frowned. Nikolai nodded. Ludmila reluctantly bobbed her head.

"Who's Nadia?" Roman said blankly.

They told him then. About the councils that governed the world of magic. About the prophecy concerning Mae. About the clashes she and the others had already had with the Dark Council and the Sorcerer King and their most recent encounter with Barquiel's devils in the crypt.

"You're the son of the Sorcerer King?" Roman asked Nikolai, aghast.

Nikolai grimaced. "I prefer to call myself the son of Gabriela Stanisic."

Julius flashed him an approving look.

Roman turned to Vlad, his face ashen. "I can't believe you're the son of Katarina and Ilmon."

Vlad froze. Tarang's ears pricked forward and backward.

CHAPTER THIRTY-ONE

Nikolai stared. *Ilmon?*

"What did you just say?!" Vlad rasped.

The name Roman had mentioned seemed to mean something to Brimstone. The fox turned to Mae.

Her eyes widened as she took part in an exchange only she and the familiar could hear. "Oh!"

Vlad's gaze snapped to her. "What?"

"Ilmon is the first incubus and the King of Incubi and Succubi," Mae said in a stunned voice. "Brim remembers him!"

Roman swallowed, his expression growing dazed as he stared at Vlad. "Katarina only mentioned that he was an important figure in the Underworld."

The color had drained from Vlad's face. Tarang whimpered worriedly and pressed against his leg.

"Eleanora never mentioned Katarina had told her the name of the incubus who sired a child with her," Budimir muttered.

An awkward look danced across Roman's face.

"Katarina had written that part down herself," he confessed reluctantly. "She masked that line with a spell only a powerful Fire Magic user could undo."

Ludmila rapped her cane sharply on the floor. "So, the one who seduced my daughter was the King of Incubi?!"

Roman's cheeks reddened a little. "She didn't exactly go into the details." He hesitated before fixing Vlad with a resolute stare. "She told Eleanora that she wanted whoever inherited her journal to be friends with her child." He faltered and glanced at Mae. "I'm not too sure how I feel about that now."

"What?" Vlad said in a dangerous voice.

Nikolai narrowed his eyes. The way Roman had looked at Mae didn't sit well with him either, for some reason.

"Can you tell us what happened after you were kidnapped?" Mae interjected hastily.

Budimir's face grew stormy when Roman described what Barquiel had done to him. Tension sparked the air as he related the conversation he'd overheard between Oscar and Dietrich when they'd thought he wasn't listening and the exchange Barquiel and Oscar had had outside his cell yesterday.

Vlad narrowed his eyes. "Hellfire Magic?"

"That's what they're after?" Mae said dazedly. "They need Hellfire Magic to unlock the *Book of Shadows?!*"

Dread tightened Nikolai's chest. "Does that mean they've already found it?"

He met Mae's gaze, his fear reflected in her eyes.

"I don't know." Roman watched them worriedly. "What's the *Book of Shadows*?"

Mae told him what they'd learned of the *Book of Light* and the *Book of Shadows* following their encounter with the Dark Council in Philadelphia.

"The soul of the first Sorcerer King is in the *Book of Shadows*?!" Roman gasped.

Mae nodded. "We think Vedran wants his soul for some reason." She clenched her jaw. "What that reason is we still don't know."

Brimstone lifted his head from where he lay at Mae's feet, his face alert. Nikolai startled when Alastair squawked out a warning on his shoulder. Tarang rose on all fours and snarled.

The building started to shake.

※

MAE JUMPED TO HER FEET, HER PULSE QUICKENING AS she scanned the windows. "Is it an attack?!"

Brimstone's crimson gaze followed hers. *I don't think so.*

Mae silently cast *Nullify*. She frowned as the tremors intensified.

Brimstone was right. There were no black magic users nearby.

It's an earthquake. A low growl vibrated through the fox's chest. *But it feels...unnatural.*

Plaster dust rained down upon their heads. Movement on the ceiling caught Mae's eye. She cursed and blocked Cortes with a barrier as a chandelier came crashing down toward him.

"We should get out of here!" Nikolai yelled.

They erected shields as they made their way out of the suite, Mae and the others protecting Vlad's bodyguards and Cortes and Budimir's men while they all headed for the fire escape. A crack tore up the wall of the stairwell when they started down the steps.

Alarm twisted Mae's stomach. *"Contain!"*

The spell flooded her veins with heat as it exploded around her. It unfurled, spreading through the hotel and down to the foundations of the building. She clenched her teeth as she tried to hold together the spreading fissures.

Shit! It's not enough!

Something brushed against her magic. Mae looked over at Roman, startled.

Power was building inside him.

Bright flames burst into life in his and Filomena's eyes. Their cores ignited with a thump she could have sworn she heard.

"Fire Fusion!" Roman invoked.

Fire Magic bloomed around him and his familiar. It whooshed up and down the building, sparing living flesh and flammables. Budimir stared at his grandson, stunned.

A proud expression danced across Ludmila's face. "Now, that's what I'm talking about!"

Blood pounded in Mae's veins when she felt Roman's conjuration melt metal and bricks into a mixture that filled the expanding cracks like glue and rapidly solidified.

They made it out of the hotel in time to see a crevice tear down the main road and swallow several vehicles in its path. The overhead lines of a cable car snapped as it plunged into the gulf, the driver's eyes round with terror behind the windshield.

"*Levitate!*" Mae shouted.

Crimson magic flickered in Brimstone's pupils and around Hellreaver as their bond amplified her power. The cable car and the vehicles reappeared from the abyss inside shimmering, red spheres, the screams of their passengers drowned out by the chaos spreading across the city.

Mae clenched her teeth and carefully deposited them in an area unaffected by the destruction the earthquake was wreaking. She widened her stance as the ground continued quaking violently beneath them, her heart racing at what she sensed deep inside the earth.

Magic was bubbling underneath Prague. Magic that was out of control. Her eyes widened.

That's—

"Shit!" Nikolai cursed, his face reflecting the same realization that had just struck her. "It's Hellfire Magic!"

"What?!" Ludmila gasped, horrified.

As if to prove his claim, a tongue of dark red flame licked the edges of the crevasse some hundred feet ahead. Explosions ripped through nearby streets and buildings as Hellfire Magic shattered gas mains and pipelines.

Mae's stomach roiled. *We have to stop it! But how?!*

Could Negate *work?!* Brimstone snarled.

It might. She scowled. *But this Hellfire Magic is so widespread I don't know if my spell will cover the whole city!*

Brimstone looked over at Nikolai. *Then how about you use someone who can focus it just where it needs to go?*

Mae's pulse stuttered. *You're right! I can try tapping into his core to direct our magic!*

"Nikolai, I need you to channel my spell into this Hellfire Magic!" she yelled.

CHAPTER THIRTY-TWO

"What?!" he spluttered.

"I'll explain later!" Mae's gaze shifted to Roman. "Come with us! Your Fire Magic might be of use too! Vlad, Ludmila, Julius. Stay here and see what you can do to minimize the damage to the area!"

"I'm only letting you boss me around 'cause you're the Witch Queen," Ludmila grumbled.

The Vissarion matriarch and her escort started erecting shields around the neighboring structures. Vlad watched forlornly while Mae made for the breach in the road with Nikolai and Roman.

Heat warmed her flesh when she stopped on the edge of the rift. Mae frowned at the Hellfire Magic boiling and hissing some hundred feet below them. Smoke from the nearby fires engulfed the road, concealing them from curious eyes.

"Brim, Hellreaver. Transform!"

The familiar and the weapon whooshed into their true shapes.

"I'm gonna need your powers to do this," she told them grimly.

Does this mean I get to play hero again?! Hellreaver asked excitedly.

Brimstone sighed at the weapon. *Our powers are yours to do with as you wish, my witch.*

Nikolai's face tightened with determination. "I think I understand what you want to try."

"Me too," Roman mumbled. He recoiled when Hellfire Magic bloomed around Nikolai and Alastair, the crow's feathers crackling with eerie flames. "Wait! How did you—?!"

"It was because of what you did to the nexus with your Fire Magic." A muscle jumped in Nikolai's cheek. "When you forced Filomena into it, your fused powers merged with white magic and created a way for Hellfire Magic to leak into the Earth. It entered my core since I was the next person to touch the nexus."

Mae blinked. *Oh. So, that's what that crack he felt was. A fracture line between the place where Azazel sealed Hellfire Magic and our realm!*

It explains what we sensed when we were at the headquarters of the Council of the Moon, Brimstone huffed.

"What?!" Roman looked wildly at the destruction around them, the blood draining from his face. Flames and fumes obscured the sky. The screams renting the air grew in number even as they listened. "You mean I —*I'm responsible for all of this?!*"

Mae shook her head. "No, Roman." She squeezed his shoulder, her voice hard. "There was no way you could have predicted this would happen. And neither did the Dark Council. I'm certain this wasn't part of their plan. Otherwise, they would have tried to find a way to inject a nexus with Fire Magic to obtain Hellfire Magic." She faltered. "It seems they thought the only way to get their hands on it was through a Fire Magic user's core."

"Mae is right," Nikolai said. "None of this is on you, Roman. You were only trying to save yourself and Filomena."

Roman swallowed convulsively, still upset at the revelation despite their reassurances. He gasped when the earth shifted violently around them. The crevasse expanded.

"Let's get to it!" Mae said hurriedly. She knelt on the perimeter of the gulf, Nikolai and Roman framing her. "See if you guys can connect your magic to that Hellfire!"

Nikolai bobbed his head. The flames around him and Alastair crackled and sparked as he focused their powers. A jet of black and crimson fire arced out of his hands and slammed into the inferno below.

Mae's pulse quickened. *Yes!*

The sorcerer grunted, his jaw tight. Her stomach clenched.

Damn! It looks like he'll only be able to sustain the link for a short time!

Roman brought his Fire Magic forth and connected it to the pit of Hellfire, perspiration beading his face. Filomena's casque quivered violently with effort where she clung to his shoulder.

Mae drew on her powers and placed her hands on their backs. Brimstone and Hellreaver's energies bolstered her magic as she invoked the spell.

"*NEGATE!*"

A crimson tempest burst around them as her powers expanded outward, the currents lifting nearby debris into the air. Mae focused the conjuration through Nikolai and Roman's cores and down the tethers that connected them to the firestorm ripping through the foundations of the city.

Nikolai and Roman screamed when the Hellfire Magic fought back, their eyes and mouths spewing black and red flames and their cores flickering dangerously where she'd tapped into the source of their powers.

"*Soul Shield!*" Mae ground out as Azazel's powerful magic raced up the bond linking it to the sorcerers and tried to consume her. "*Multiply!*"

The blaze roared angrily as it slammed into the powerful cages protecting all their cores and those of their familiars. It twisted around and followed the only path it could, down into the Earth again.

Which was exactly where *Negate* awaited it.

Mae's heart thumped painfully against her ribs as her magic slowly suppressed the hellish conflagration sparking across thousands of feet of rock and earth. Brimstone and Hellreaver pressed against her, boosting her rapidly depleting stamina.

Shit! This thing is a beast. No wonder Azazel sealed it! Her breath locked in her throat when she caught a glimpse of the nexus. *Our father created that?!*

Tears pricked Mae's eyes as Na Ri's presence fluttered inside her, her original incarnation equally awed by what she could see through her inner vision.

The nexus was beautiful.

Mae's pulse stuttered when she detected the anomaly within it. "That's the crack!"

"We don't have enough power to close it right now," Brimstone warned. *"Besides, we need to be physically closer to the irregularity to even attempt it."*

She clenched her jaw. The fox was right. All they could do was stabilize the core and the burning ley lines connected to it.

The violent quakes shaking the city started to subside as *Negate* sucked away at the last of the Hellfire Magic that had invaded its vast substructure. The tremors ended with an abruptness that made Mae's ears ring. Nikolai and Roman's labored pants finally reached her as the blood roaring in her skull abated.

Nikolai wiped soot and perspiration from his brow, his Hellfire Magic fading. "Did we do it?!"

Mae smiled shakily. "Yeah. You guys did good."

"Thank God," Roman mumbled.

He fell back on his bottom, raised his face to sky, and closed his eyes, pale with relief.

Nikolai stiffened. Horror leached the color from his skin. He looked toward the river.

"Marlena!"

CHAPTER THIRTY-THREE

Smoke obscured the sky in the direction of the island where the headquarters of the Council of the Moon was located. Nikolai's pulse raced as he tapped the brakes and sent the SUV careening sharply around a corner.

Mae and Vlad cursed when they were jolted violently against the rear passenger door. Roman disappeared under Tarang with a muffled, "Oof!"

"This is like Philadelphia all over again!" Vlad said darkly as he straightened. He grabbed Roman's arm and tugged him out from under the tiger. "This asshole has no concept of road safety!"

Mae made a face. Roman wiped white fur from his mouth and looked anxiously for Filomena. The chameleon squeezed up Tarang's flank and leapt onto her sorcerer's shoulder, her hiss of annoyance loud.

Nikolai glanced at Julius where he was hanging on to the seat beside him. "Any news?"

"I can't get in touch with Marlena or Klara," the

sorcerer said bitterly, his knuckles white on his cell phone.

Nikolai's stomach plummeted. His gaze found the dark sky once more.

Please, let them be okay!

He hadn't realized how much he'd come to care for his aunt, his cousin, and the entire family he'd made at the Council of the Moon until the reality of losing them had rocked his world in the aftermath of the earthquake.

"The communication towers are down," Mae said. "Marlena and your family are strong, Nikolai. I'm sure they're fine."

Nikolai met her gaze in the rearview mirror, grateful for her quiet strength. His core still tingled where her magic had connected with his powers. It felt strange. Intimate, even.

He clenched his jaw, ashamed of where his thoughts had strayed. *I can't think about things like that right now!*

Alastair's feathers gently ruffled his cheek.

The island finally appeared when they shot onto a bridge and took an exit.

"Son of a—!" Julius swore.

Fear drenched Nikolai in a cold sweat. Mae's fingers sank into his headrest as she leaned forward to peer through the windshield.

A third of the island was under water. The red blaze of a fire glowed in the center.

"The bridge is gone!" Julius barked.

Nikolai cursed and pressed on the brakes as they approached the riverside.

"Keep going!" Mae wound the rear window down and leaned out. Her pupils glowed crimson. *"Ice Fortress!"*

The river surged up on a powerful wave and froze over, forming a bridge to the island. Nikolai accelerated.

The SUV shot off the bank and landed on the makeshift overpass with a bone-jarring thud. He cursed as they skidded and started spinning violently on the ice.

"Shit!" Vlad yelled.

Heat bloomed in Nikolai's belly as the river loomed on their right. Alastair squawked.

"Moon Storm!"

Moon Magic detonated next to the SUV. The backdraft shoved them back to the center of the bridge. They cleared it seconds later, the vehicles following them slowing to navigate the frozen water with more caution than they had.

Shadows swallowed them when they entered the tree line. They emerged from the woods and came in sight of the headquarters of the Council of the Moon.

Nikolai's stomach plummeted.

The south wing was gone. Flames swallowed the central building and north wing. He scanned the figures in the garden, his heart throbbing painfully in his chest. Alastair cawed.

Nikolai's mouth went dry when he spotted what the crow had seen.

Marlena and Klara stood in the front courtyard and were directing the council's efforts to put out the fires.

Nikolai braked, jumped out of the vehicle, and rushed over to them.

Klara saw him first. "Nikolai!"

He swept the two women up in his arms and hugged them tightly, tears choking his throat. They clutched his back, their relief equally palpable as they trembled in his hold.

"I'm so glad you're safe!" Nikolai mumbled in their hair.

Klara sniffed and pulled back with a tremulous smile. "We were so worried about you!"

"The bridge." Marlena's eyes rounded in incomprehension. "We thought it was gone!"

"It is," Nikolai said grimly. "Mae created a temporary overpass."

Mae and the others joined them.

It took a couple of hours siphoning water from the river with their spells to put out the blaze that had ripped through the headquarters of the Council of the Moon. It wasn't until midafternoon that they finally managed to congregate in a conference room that had been spared by the fires and confer on what had taken place that morning.

Lines furrowed Marlena's brow as she studied Roman. "You're the young man who inherited Katarina Vissarion's Fire Magic?"

He dipped his chin.

Marlena's face tightened as she looked over at Ludmila. "What do you intend to do with the Fire Magic users Mae rescued from the Dark Council?"

"Return them to their homes, what else?" Ludmila

sighed at Marlena's incredulous stare. "I know what you're thinking, but I have no intention of…forcing Roman or anyone else under my will, like I tried to do with my daughter. That did not end well for anyone."

Vlad's face grew cool at that.

Nikolai reckoned Budimir would have shared the incubus's feelings had he been present. The Bratva general had not been best pleased when they'd left him at the hotel. It was Mae who had convinced him that, in a battle of magic, he would only be a hindrance to them.

Cortes had insisted on accompanying them, however. Seeing as this might be his only chance at getting revenge, Mae had reluctantly allowed him to come along.

Marlena eyed the Colombian presently. "Mae told me about you. I'm amazed you've survived so long." The witch drummed her fingers on the table, faint lines wrinkling her brow as her expression grew thoughtful. "She's right. There's a good chance your powers will surpass those of Raya if she does manage to fix your core. We'll have to find you a familiar in tune with your Arcane Magic, of course."

Cortes blinked. He turned to Mae. "You told her that?"

Mae shrugged. "It's the truth."

"There hasn't been an Arcane Magic user on our side for centuries," Ludmila said shrewdly. "We'll use you well, boy."

Cortes grimaced. "You know I have another day job, right?"

"Pish posh," Ludmila said dismissively. "Mark my words, the criminal underworld will go under if Vedran claims Mae's powers."

Vlad shot Cortes a commiserating glance. "Looks like you're stuck with the old hag whether you like it or not."

Ludmila narrowed her eyes at her grandson.

"So, Hellfire Magic is what they were after all along?" Klara said, ashen faced. "That's why they killed so many Fire Magic users?"

"Yeah," Mae replied grimly. "Hiding Filomena in the nexus saved Roman from that fate."

"But it also gifted Nikolai with Hellfire Magic," Marlena said stiffly. "The very magic the Dark Council is after." She cast a worried look at her nephew. "They won't stop coming after you once they find out about this."

Dread knotted Nikolai's shoulders as he stared at the floor. He swallowed, a singular truth resonating through him then.

If Raya had foreseen the powers he would eventually manifest and master, there was no way he would have escaped Budapest. His father would have chained him and kept him at his side even if he'd had to cut off his legs to do so, and Nikolai would never have awakened Mae in time for her to escape the Dark Council's clutches.

"I owe Nikolai for the fact that I did not fall into the Dark Council's hands before I knew who I was."

His head snapped up at Mae's quiet words. Her gaze

grew poignant as she watched him. It seemed she'd read his mind.

"I won't let them get their hands on you." She faltered. "And if they do. If, by some slim chance, they ever happen to capture you? Know that I will move Heaven and Earth to free you. And so will the rest of us who oppose your father."

Nikolai's heart swelled at the truth he saw reflected on her face and everyone else's.

"Yeah, it'll piss me off to no end if I win by default, Moon Boy," Vlad muttered.

Nikolai scowled.

Mae blew out a sigh. "You're such an ass."

Vlad flashed her a sinful smile.

"This ass is all yours, Princess," he drawled, his demon energy washing across the room in a wave that made several people flush. "Like I said before, you're more than welcome to touch it."

"What a douchebag," Roman said under his breath, evidently immune to the incubus's charms.

Vlad squinted. "What was that, kid?"

"The Dark Council probably knows about the Hellfire Magic that ripped through the city by now," Marlena muttered. "They'll want to find its source."

"We have to close the rift in the nexus before they do." Nikolai sat back and raked his hair with a hand, frustration churning his insides. "But how?"

"I think I might have an idea." Mae grimaced. "But—you're not going to like it."

They listened to her suggestion with mounting horror.

"Absolutely no way in Hell!" Vlad snapped.

"Are you insane?!" Ludmila barked.

"Bryony will have our guts for garters if we let you carry out such an asinine plan," Violet said grimly.

Roman swallowed, his expression ashen.

Nikolai stared at Mae, fear clashing with wild hope inside him.

"We might not make it back alive," he rasped.

Brimstone transformed. *"If anyone can do this, my witch can."* His crimson gaze probed Nikolai and Roman. *"And she will need you both to help her."*

CHAPTER THIRTY-FOUR

"Are you sure about this?" Roman asked for the tenth time.

Mae dipped her chin. "Going into the nexus is our best option to close off the source of Hellfire Magic the Dark Council will be coming after."

They were standing in the middle of the courtyard that formed the Council of the Moon's main training ground. Bar some cracks that had torn through the galleries, it had mostly been spared by the earthquakes that had wreaked havoc on the city, thanks to the Moon Magic barrier that protected it.

Roman dug his nails into his palms as he examined Mae and Nikolai's determined expressions, unease tightening his chest. "Let me come with you. I can help!"

"You're helping already, Roman," Nikolai said. "Only you have mastered this spell. You can't be both inside *and* outside it."

Roman sagged a little, knowing the sorcerer spoke the truth.

"But I've never tried *Transmigrate* on people before," he mumbled.

Mae grinned and slapped him heartily on the back. "Well, there's a first time for everything."

The kiss the Witch Queen had given him in the dungeon danced before his inner vision. Roman's face warmed.

A low growl escaped Brimstone. The fox's ears pricked as he looked to the north.

"Brim?" Mae said, puzzled.

"*Barquiel draws close,*" the fox growled.

Mae and Nikolai stiffened. Dread quickened Roman's pulse.

Julius rushed inside the arena. "We have incoming! It's the Dark Council!"

"Shit." Violet unleashed her blade, her rabbit's eyes flashing purple. "We cannot catch a break!"

"We'll erect a barrier around the building and try and keep them out for as long as we can!" Julius said.

"Stay here and watch over them with Ludmila!" Vlad told Violet and Miles.

He looked longingly at Mae before disappearing after Julius.

Mae frowned.

"We have to go," she said in a brittle voice.

Roman clenched his jaw and nodded. He led the way to the fissure in the middle of the training ground. It was where Filomena had appeared from the nexus.

Mae and Nikolai took up position over the crack and locked hands.

Brimstone whined softly. *"Be well, my witch."*

He lowered his head and carefully licked Mae's face.

She stroked his cheek, her eyes bright with emotion. "I'll be back soon."

They'd decided the fox should stay up top to tether Mae's core to the surface in case something went wrong. Hellreaver and Alastair would be going into the nexus with her and Nikolai.

Roman knelt in front of them, Filomena on his shoulder. Heat flared through his belly and across their bond as he reached for his Fire Magic. He took a deep breath, pressed his hands to the ground, and sought out the nexus.

It only took a couple of heartbeats to find it. *I can't believe it was beneath this building all along.*

White magic infused his bloodstream as he grasped a bundle of ley lines close to it. He gritted his teeth. He had never seen the nexus flicker so agitatedly before.

It must be fighting the anomaly within it!

"Get ready," Roman warned Mae and Nikolai.

They pressed their fingers to his shoulders.

"Transmigrate!" he barked.

Whiteness bloomed around the witch and the sorcerer as the spell took form. They shrank and vanished in a dazzling flash that smelled of ozone.

❄

Explosions rocked the island as the Dark Council started attacking the mansion. Vlad and Cortes came out into the exposed foyer of the Council of the Moon. The incubus's pulse raced.

Scores of black-magic sorcerers and witches levitated within dark spheres beyond the pale barrier enclosing the remains of the mansion. He ground his teeth.

He couldn't see Barquiel or Oscar.

Where are those bastards?!

Marlena and Klara's eyes glowed fiercely while they powered the Moon Magic shield deflecting the corrupt orbs being aimed at the building, their familiars and the rest of their council aiding them. Julius and several others protected them with a secondary barrier.

Movement up ahead caught Vlad's gaze. He cursed when he saw a couple of black-magic sorcerers appear inside the barrier.

"I can sense Raya's magic." Cortes scowled. "She must be warping them through!"

Tarang's hackles rose. He was staring at a shadowy corridor filled with debris on their right.

A familiar corruption danced across Vlad's skin.

"It's not just her," he spat. "There's a portal close by!"

The rubble exploded. Julius grunted when chunks of wreckage slammed into his shield.

It held.

Vlad erected a protective layer of incubus magic around Cortes as Oscar appeared through the hole with his lynx.

"Don't move from here!" he warned the Colombian. "I can't say what will happen if you do!"

Cortes bobbed his head grimly.

Vlad worked out the knots in his neck and reached for the demonic energy in his core. Crimson exploded in Tarang's eyes as he fell into step beside him.

More Dark Council members were materializing inside the pale barrier. The Vissarions' Fire Magic users engaged them.

Vlad focused on Oscar's scowling face. "Tarang?" The tiger looked at him. He touched his familiar's head and flashed him a savage smile. "Don't hold back!"

Tarang's pupils dilated. The familiar snarled, a red haze exploding around him as they both let go of the tight rein they'd maintained over their abilities since the night they'd lost control and killed Budimir's son.

Vlad shuddered as the demonic blood he had inherited from his father ignited his veins fully and spilled out onto his diamond-edged swords in a powerful, crimson blast.

Oscar faltered, his expression growing wary. He stopped and cast a barrage of dark orbs at them.

Vlad smashed through them with his blades, the corrupt spheres fizzling into dissipating wisps of darkness under the influence of his incubus power.

Oscar cursed.

Vlad moved, Tarang a white blur beside him.

Oscar cried out when a diamond-edged blade scored his flank. Drabek screeched as Tarang's claws found her face.

The sorcerer's eyes widened in incomprehension. "How—?!"

He deflected Vlad's second sword an inch from his throat, his own blade quivering as he grunted with effort. Drabek spat at Tarang, pupils oozing black magic and blood dripping from her wounds.

Vlad sneered. "Not bad, asshole."

He pressed down. His blade nicked Oscar's neck.

"I'm stronger than you!" the sorcerer snarled, his knuckles whitening as he pushed back. "How can a mongrel with mixed blood—?!"

He choked when Vlad kneed him viciously in the gut.

The sorcerer skidded backward, his fingers raking the floor to stop himself from falling over. His face filled with murderous intent. He swore and straightened, barely catching Drabek as the lynx sailed toward him with a pained whimper.

Tarang had batted the familiar away with a giant paw, leaving more slashes in her flank.

"You bastards!" Oscar hissed.

Vlad grinned. "It takes one to know one."

"Vlad!" Cortes barked out in warning.

Vlad moved a fraction too late to avoid the attack coming at him. Heat flared on his left flank as the spell bomb glanced off his body, drawing a grunt from his throat and a roar of outrage from Tarang.

Shit! That was close!

He whirled around to face the enemy who had cast the attack. Ice filled his veins.

Raya Medeiros pushed her hood back as she

emerged from thin air, her pupils and fingers aglow with the same amber magic that sparked in the eyes of the black mamba coiled around her arm.

Cortes swore.

Raya's gaze found him. Her expression turned ugly.

"I heard a rat was spotted in our hideout." She sneered. "It seems like I'm going to have to teach you a lesson again, *nephew!*" She glowered at Vlad. "But let me take care of this mongrel first."

CHAPTER THIRTY-FIVE

Mae.

Warmth surrounded Mae, a haven that pulsed faintly, like a comforting heartbeat. She floated within the pale, undefined space, safe and at peace.

Mae.

Mae frowned. She burrowed deeper into the fluffy clouds surrounding her like cotton candy, determined to ignore the voice trying to drag her out of her snug bed.

Wake up, Mae.

"Go away," Mae mumbled.

Low laughter reached her and danced through her ears, the sound strangely musical.

I see both my daughters are sound sleepers.

Mae's heart throbbed. Her eyelids fluttered.

She struggled to fight the drowsiness dragging her under once more, conscious she had to wake up and try and make sense of the words she'd just heard. The words that were making a sea of sadness well up from deep within her.

Fingers grasped her shoulders, their heat searing her skin. Someone yanked her out of her warm cocoon.

"Wake up, Mae!" Nikolai shouted close by.

Mae's eyes snapped open.

The sorcerer was kneeling above her, his face full of dread and his pupils blazing with magic. Alastair squawked worriedly on his shoulder. Hellreaver floated beside them, the weapon humming agitatedly.

He shot into her arms. *My witch!*

Mae blinked and hugged him.

Nikolai sagged, tension visibly draining out of him.

She sat up slowly, Hellreaver still clinging to her. "What—what happened?"

Her eyes rounded. They were inside a dazzling space churning with magic. Waves of pure energy washed across her skin and ruffled her hair as she climbed to her feet, Nikolai helping her.

"Wait!" Mae breathed. She'd just noticed the pale rivers pouring into the place they stood in from high above. "Is this the nexus?!"

Nikolai nodded. Sparks danced around him and Alastair, their cores blazing as the magic inside the nexus amplified their strength.

Mae twisted on her heels. "It's big."

She couldn't see the boundaries of the nexus.

Nikolai hesitated, his expression wary as he followed her gaze. "I think it's more a metaphysical space than a real one."

"Oh." Mae blinked. "That would make sense."

"The crack is this way."

Nikolai took her hand and headed into the whiteness, as if he were scared to let her go.

Tingles of awareness shot up Mae's arm. She swallowed self-consciously. The way Hellreaver looked at her told her the weapon had sensed the direction her thoughts had just taken.

Her heart slammed against her ribs as she recalled the voice she'd heard. *Was that Ran Soyun?!*

Na Ri's presence surged within her, confirming her suspicion. Mae looked around.

Is it because this place is filled with the magic Azazel gifted our mother?!

Something caught her gaze up ahead. A darkness amidst the light. The phenomenon grew into a black scar some fifty feet long and ten feet wide.

It had ripped through the heart of the nexus and was spewing Hellfire Magic into the Earth.

Mae shuddered when her core resonated with the hellish energy throbbing from the crimson and black flames.

Master, Hellreaver mumbled.

She glanced at the weapon, surprised.

Hellreaver whined. *Master is close!*

Mae flinched.

"What is it?" Nikolai said.

She stared at the anomaly, her chest tight. *Is this thing connected to the level of Hell where my father is?!*

"Hellreaver says he can feel Azazel," she replied grimly.

Nikolai startled. "What?!"

Mae ignored the sudden longing growing in her heart and clenched her jaw. "Let's close it, like we planned."

The sorcerer hesitated. "Are you sure?"

Mae met his anxious gaze with a calm expression. "I hope to meet my father one day. But not like this."

Nikolai watched her for a beat longer before nodding. "Okay."

He took a shallow breath, let go of her hand, and stepped up to the edge of the abyss. Hellfire Magic flared on his fingertips. Alastair's wings detonated with a scarlet blaze laced with inky threads.

They focused their powers on the crack.

Mae reached for her core. A red haze exploded across Hellreaver as he boosted her magic. She touched Nikolai's back and invoked the spell bubbling in her veins.

"*Sever!*"

Her heart thumped against her ribs as she felt the spell traverse Nikolai and Alastair's cores. The sorcerer shuddered. He ground his teeth, sweat beading his face as she used him and his familiar as a conduit to close the rift.

The fissure trembled.

"It's...not enough!" Nikolai gasped after a moment.

Mae cursed. Her hair lifted around her as she grasped the crimson blaze churning deep within her body and drew upon it fully.

Nikolai grunted. Alastair's wings quivered violently.

They can't take much more of this, my witch! Hellreaver said worriedly after a minute. *Their cores will crack!*

Fear gripped Mae at her weapon's warning. She started withdrawing her power from Nikolai and Alastair.

A voice reached her then.

One that rooted her limbs to the ground and made her soul tremble, just like her heart had done upon hearing Ran Soyun.

"Na—*Na Ri?!*" someone shouted dimly somewhere below.

Mae stared into the inferno of Hellfire Magic.

The flames thinned, revealing a shimmering portal to some kind of cave. Her stomach plummeted as she stared through the narrow window. A haggard, horned demon with crimson pupils and a tattered robe was looking straight up at her.

The demon's face brightened. "Na Ri!"

Mae blinked. *"Fa—Father?!"*

Master! Hellreaver blubbered.

Relief flooded Azazel's eyes when he saw the weapon. "I'm glad you found your mistress, Hellreaver!"

The weapon whined, a sound of sorrow.

The demon studied Nikolai and the Hellfire Magic blazing in his blind gaze and that of his familiar.

He frowned. "I wish we could talk longer, daughter, but it seems you have a situation!"

Mae dipped her head, tongue-tied. She recalled what Alicia had told her of Azazel. How Ran Soyun and Na Ri's deaths had driven the demon so mad with grief none could reason with him, and how he'd wandered aimlessly through the deepest parts of Hell for eons.

Is that why he looks so gaunt, like he hasn't slept in years?

The portal wavered. Panic clenched her belly.

"Father!"

Azazel's voice came brokenly through the roaring blaze. "I—teach—spell—!"

The window reappeared. Azazel's pupils flared with power as he raised his hands toward her.

Mae's breath locked in her lungs when his magic connected with her core and detonated inside her mind. The conjuration appeared in her subconscious, so bright it scorched her soul.

She opened her mouth and invoked it. *"Chaos Seal!"*

The anomaly started shrinking, white magic sparking at the jagged edges as the nexus finally won the battle against the otherworldly power that had almost overwhelmed it.

Azazel's portal flickered as the rift started to close.

"We will meet again, daughter!" he shouted, his eyes bright with conviction.

Mae swallowed, her vision blurring with tears. "My name is Mae now, father! Hana Mae Jin!"

Pleasure danced in Azazel's loving gaze. "Mae. I like it, daughter!"

Mae froze when the portal shuddered and winked out. She closed her eyes tightly, overcome with a grief so deep she felt it would drive her into the ground.

Come, my witch. Hellreaver nudged her gently, his voice quivering. *We still have work to do.*

The weapon sniffed.

Mae swallowed and nodded. "Thanks, Hell."

The hellish power leaking into the Earth finally abated when the fissure closed. She retracted her magic from Nikolai and steadied the sorcerer as he swayed.

Hellreaver caught Alastair when he plummeted from Nikolai's shoulder. The weapon lowered the limp crow to the floor of the nexus, just as Mae did his barely conscious sorcerer.

Will they be okay? Hellreaver said worriedly. *Their heartbeats are really slow.*

"Yeah."

Mae slumped cross-legged on the ground and leaned her hands behind her, feeling drained all of a sudden.

"We're in the nexus after all," she mumbled. "We just need to give them time to recover."

To her surprise, the white magic around her slowly replenished her depleted core too.

Well, Mom was the first white magic user, after all. Maybe the nexus can sense this.

Hellreaver squirmed next to her.

"What is it?" Mae murmured.

The weapon indicated the unconscious sorcerer with a tilt of a blade. *You could always kiss him awake, like in fairytales.* His lecherous tone brightened. *Better still, you could do all the naughty things you've been fantasizing about doing to—*Hellreaver stilled at her glare. *I'll...just go hover over there, shall I?*

"You do that," Mae snapped.

CHAPTER THIRTY-SIX

Heat flooded Roman's veins. "*Ignite!*"

Filomena's claws sank into his shoulder as Fire Magic detonated outside the golden barrier they stood within. It ripped through the training ground and smashed into the black-magic sorcerers and witches whose shields were too weak to hold against the attack.

The men and women screamed as flames raced up their clothes and reddened their flesh.

"*Inferno!*" Ludmila invoked, jaw tight and Brimstone hovering protectively over her.

Her salamander's pupils ignited. The blaze that exploded from the tip of her cane sent cracks racing across the stone beneath them as it arrowed toward Barquiel.

The demon moved nimbly out of the path of her attack, his expression almost bored. Lines furrowed his brow when the spell zoomed around the arena and came at him once more.

Ludmila smirked.

Barquiel deflected *Inferno* with his broadsword. It engulfed his blade. He snarled, corruption blossoming around him. Ludmila's Fire Magic dissipated, the flames smothered by the vile energy.

The witch cursed.

Roman's heart raced with trepidation as he glanced across the arena. The barrier Violet and Miles had erected was the only thing that was still holding against the Dark Council's relentless attacks. Klara and the other Moon Magic users were feeding it with their powers where they'd retreated to their side.

Marlena, Julius, and the Vissarions' Fire Magic users faced off against Oscar at the east end of the arena, their shields quivering as his orbs slammed into them.

The only other ones outside the barrier were Vlad and Cortes.

The two men were engaged in a deadly battle with a woman wielding amber spell bombs. Blood dripped from Cortes's many wounds as he clasped one of Vlad's diamond-edged swords, the blade blurring in his hands like he'd used it for years. Tarang shielded him from the witch's blasts.

Movement in the sky captured Roman's attention. His stomach roiled when he saw the clouds moving across it. A dark pall soon covered the training ground. The clouds started spinning ominously, sparks of black lightning crackling amidst them.

Violet's chest heaved with her ragged breaths where she maintained the golden shield protecting them. "Shit!"

"We could really do with Mae and Nikolai's help right about now!" Miles grunted.

Sweat dripped down the sorcerer's face as he poured magic into the barrier.

Roman stared at Barquiel. *He's the one doing that!*

Black lightning cracked the sky. The bolt connected with the demon's blade and arced toward Ludmila.

A crimson wave exploded from Brimstone as his tails vibrated violently. Barquiel's attack crashed into the red sphere blossoming around him and Ludmila.

The ground caved beneath the nine-tailed fox. He snarled, flecks of drool falling from his jowls as he bowed under the pressure of the attack, his pupils aglow with demonic power. His legs slowly straightened.

Barquiel scowled.

❋

A RED RIVULET DRIPPED DOWN VLAD'S THIGH WHERE ONE of Raya's attacks had carved a gash in his flesh. Had it not been for the veneer of incubus energy coating his skin, he would have lost the limb.

He wiped sweat and blood from his face before shooting a hard glance at Cortes. "Together!"

Cortes nodded, his face an icy mask of resolve. He followed Vlad's lead and charged Raya, the black blade dancing in his hands as he batted away at the barrage of spell bombs she aimed at them.

Even though the Colombian could not wield magic, he more than made up for it with his animal instincts and his fighting skills. Vlad understood why the seer had been so scared of her nephew and had attempted to get rid of him when he was too young to defend himself.

Had Cortes been able to tap into his Arcane Magic right now, she would have been a bloodied corpse on the ground.

Tarang snagged the back of Raya's left ankle with his claws. The witch screeched in pain and fury as her flesh was ripped to shreds, exposing her Achilles tendon. She whirled around and cast a spell bomb at the tiger.

Vlad deflected the orb a few inches from his familiar's left eye.

"Stay away from my tiger, bitch!" he hissed at Raya.

Incubus magic boomed around him as he drew on his demonic core. Tarang roared, pupils radiating a deadly scarlet light.

Raya cursed as Vlad darted closer, the edge of his blade skimming past her face again and again. The witch's eyes flashed amber as she raised a hand to blast him with a spell.

Something glinted at the edge of Vlad's vision.

A savage grin stretched his lips. *Gotcha!*

Raya's look of incomprehension froze. Cortes's dagger sailed straight and true through the air, nicked her ear lobe, and sliced her black mamba's head clean off. The snake's body convulsed and sprayed her cloak and face with blood even as the knife pierced a column opposite them.

The seer reached up and touched her cheek in a

daze. Her eyes rounded when her fingertips came away crimson. *"No!"*

Her frightened gaze found her familiar's head where it flopped at her feet. A choked sound left her with her next breath.

"It sucks, doesn't it?" Cortes said inches from Raya's face. "Having your familiar die?"

Raya's shocked gaze dropped from her nephew's face to the black blade that had stabbed her chest and skewered her heart before exiting her back.

Cortes stared into Raya's eyes and twisted the blade. "At least I've done you the courtesy of killing you quickly, aunt."

Blood spurted from the witch's mouth.

Cortes ripped the sword out of her body and dispassionately wiped away the crimson jet that had sprayed his chin as she folded limply at his feet.

Vlad joined him. Cortes handed him his sword wordlessly.

The floor trembled violently beneath them.

Vlad's heart lurched as a familiar power raised the hairs of his nape. He twisted around and stared toward the center of the training ground.

Mae!

CHAPTER THIRTY-SEVEN

THE SOUND OF DETONATING SPELL BOMBS FILLED MAE'S ears as she burst out of the crack in the middle of the arena with Nikolai, the globe of white magic that had returned them to the surface fizzing out around them.

Warmth pulsed through her body as Brimstone's core resonated brightly with hers.

"My witch!"

Relief laced the fox's voice behind her. Mae whirled around. Her heart stuttered.

Rage blossomed within her.

Blood dripped down Brimstone's flanks and his enormous head where he crouched protectively over Ludmila. The Vissarion matriarch was leaning heavily on her cane in his shadow, the witch's chest heaving with her breaths while her salamander clung limply to her shoulder.

Those two are almost out of magic! Mae's pulse quickened when her gaze found Violet, Miles, and Klara where they were barely managing to manifest the divine shield protecting Roman and the sorcerers and witches on their side. *So are they!*

She scanned the area for the source of the corrupt energy washing across her skin and spotted Oscar engaging Marlena and Julius to the far left.

"*Watch out!*" Roman shouted.

Hellreaver shot out of her hand and placed himself between her and the black lightning dropping from the sky.

Mae's eyes widened. *No!*

Heat scorched her veins and blazed across her bond with Hellreaver and Brimstone. *Devour* bloomed above the weapon a heartbeat before Barquiel's attack could smash into him.

The spell swallowed the corrupt bolt with a *glomp*.

Yeesh! Hellreaver shuddered as he returned to her side. *I thought I was toast there for a second!*

Barquiel roared angrily where he floated high above the amphitheater.

Mae clenched her jaw. A crimson storm burst around her as she levitated in the air.

"How about you go take care of your brother while I get rid of this asshole?!" she growled at Nikolai.

The sorcerer's pupils brightened with white magic. "With pleasure."

He made his way toward the other side of the amphitheater with Alastair.

Barquiel shot back to a safe distance when Mae rose to his level. He glanced at the floor of the arena, fury and confusion warring in his scarlet gaze. "Where's the Hellfire Magic?! I could smell it a moment ago!"

"Oh, that?" Mae cocked her head. "Azazel helped me seal it."

Barquiel recoiled, his pupils flaring. "What?!"

"You heard me right the first time, shit for brains." She cracked her knuckles, her eyes shrinking into slits. "Now, how about I rearrange your face for what you did to my fox?"

❋

OSCAR'S LOATHSOME GAZE FOUND NIKOLAI AS HE approached.

"Stand down," Nikolai told Marlena and Julius.

His aunt and the sorcerer hesitated, blood dripping from the wounds Oscar had inflicted upon them with his blade, their familiars' eyes aglow with Moon Magic.

"Trust me," Nikolai said. "I've got this."

Marlena blinked at what she read on his face. She dipped her head and placed a warning hand on Julius's arm.

Oscar sneered. "You think you can fight me on your own?!"

Nikolai met his brother's gaze steadily. "I *know* I can."

He was surprised at how calm he felt. Maybe it was because his core felt stable. More stable than it had been in weeks. Months even.

It seemed going to the nexus had granted him the power to balance the three types of magic now inhabiting his body. And not just that.

He noted Oscar's wounds and those of his lynx. "I

see Vlad managed to do some damage. Shame he couldn't finish the job."

"Hey, don't think I didn't hear that, asshole!" the incubus shouted from across the way.

Nikolai shot a mocking smile at him. His gaze found Cortes where the man stood beside the incubus. Surprise jolted him when he registered who was lying at the Colombian's feet.

Raya Medeiros stared sightlessly back at him from across the arena, her body lying limply in an expanding, crimson pool.

"Our father won't be happy about that," Nikolai murmured.

Oscar's head snapped around as he followed his gaze. His eyes rounded. An outraged roar left his throat. Drabek screeched.

Corruption surged in the lynx's eyes and around Oscar.

Nikolai was ready for the attack. Heat streamed through his and Alastair's cores, their blended magic flowing smoothly in their veins.

"*Moon Fire.*"

Oscar gasped as a violent surge of pale flames wrapped around him and Drabek and lifted them into the air. He cursed, the black orbs hovering above his hands rapidly absorbed by the glittering currents.

An explosion boomed across the arena. Nikolai looked over to where the sound had come from.

Barquiel had smashed into the ground of the amphitheater. A bellow of pure wrath escaped the demon as he rose, debris falling from his wings.

Mae's figure painted a red streak in the air as she zoomed toward him at supersonic speed. Her fist struck his jaw with enough force to make the air ripple and drive Violet, Miles, and Klara several feet across the ground behind their barrier.

Ludmila waved her cane with a triumphant smile where she leaned against Brimstone's leg. "Oh, well done!"

Oscar's voice reached Nikolai.

"Impossible!" the sorcerer snarled. "How is she managing to do that?!"

Nikolai's heart lightened as he watched Mae pummel Barquiel, the demon's blood coating her fists with thick, dark smears. "She and I got a boost of magic."

Oscar glowered. "What do you mean?!"

Nikolai bared his teeth in a cold smile. "Why don't I show you?"

Hellfire Magic flared in his belly. It sparked through his bloodstream and poured out of his skin. Alastair's wings detonated with flames where he gripped his shoulder.

Oscar blanched. "That's—!"

The spell emerged from the new repertoire of conjurations Nikolai seemed to have absorbed into his mind when he had been recovering in the nexus.

"Hell Flare."

A black and crimson firestorm engulfed the arena, so fierce it melted metal. The spell spared everyone but Oscar, his lynx, and Barquiel. The sorcerer and the demon screamed as it consumed their powers, Drabek screeching so loudly Nikolai's ears throbbed.

He stiffened when a familiar, sinister magic washed across him.

Mae's shield bloomed above them a heartbeat before a dark sphere exploded within Hell Flare where it filled the sky above the arena. The orb expanded into a doorway that pulled Oscar, Drabek, and Barquiel through to the void beyond.

Nikolai clenched his jaw. *Vedran!*

Mae scowled as the black-magic portal vanished.

Nikolai ended Hell Flare seconds later.

A heavy silence descended around them, the hush broken by the crackles of the fresh fires that had engulfed the remains of the mansion in the wake of the Dark Council's attack.

Brimstone limped toward Mae as she glided to the ground. *"My witch!"*

He shrank into his small form and jumped into her waiting arms.

"Brim!" She hugged him tightly to her chest and squeezed her eyes shut, her voice trembling. "Are you hurt bad?!"

The fox huffed and licked her face, magic sparking across his body. His wounds were already healing.

They regrouped in the middle of the training ground.

"That spell was amazing," Mae told Nikolai, her eyes glittering with admiration.

His belly tightened at her praise. He smiled.

Mae blinked. Her cheeks reddened.

"Hey, stop making puppy eyes at her," Vlad snapped.

Nikolai lowered his brows at the incubus.

"Still," Mae mumbled. "I was *so* close to smashing Barquiel's nose."

Violet squinted at her downcast expression. "I seriously hope you weren't thinking of asking him to hold back on that spell so you could break a demon's face?"

Mae looked faintly guilty at their suspicious stares.

"It would only have been for a couple of seconds," she said defensively.

Groans rose across the arena. Nikolai sighed. So did Vlad. Even Cortes looked at Mae like she had a screw loose.

A crash came from behind them. They whirled around.

The mansion was collapsing.

Marlena sagged as she gazed upon the ruins of her headquarters.

"I think you need to relocate," Ludmila told the witch.

CHAPTER THIRTY-EIGHT

Sunlight flickered across Mae's eyelids. She pulled the covers over her head and snuggled deeper into the bed.

I sense trouble, my witch.

Mae blinked her eyes open and almost swallowed her tongue.

Brimstone's face was an inch from hers.

She bolted upright, the bedspread flying into the air. Brimstone straightened from where he'd been crouching next to her pillow.

Mae pressed a hand to her chest and glowered at the fox. "Like, seriously, *stop doing that!*"

Hellreaver snorted in his sleep.

What's happening? he mumbled drowsily against her chest.

There is a man in Mae's mother's bedroom, Brimstone growled.

Hellreaver quivered, alarmed.

Mae jumped out of bed and cast *Nullify* before

scanning the house, her pulse racing. Bar Noah's core, she couldn't detect any other magic user in her mother's home. She frowned and started briskly for the door.

"Do you know who it is, Brim?!"

It's that Fusanaga guy, Brimstone replied, outraged.

Mae froze. Her gaze dropped to the fox where he padded beside her. "Huh?"

Brimstone stopped and sat on his haunches.

Mae blinked, confused. "By Fusanaga, you mean...?"

Itou Fusanaga. Your new funeral director.

Mae's eyes bulged. Her racing mind rapidly connected the dots when she recalled what Ryu had told her about Mr. Fusanaga frequently visiting their home for dinner.

Wait. Could it be—?!

She swallowed. "I—I think I know what's going on."

Brimstone looked suitably impressed. *You do?*

Mae nodded jerkily. She sneaked out of her room, tip-toed past her grandmother's bedroom, and rapped her knuckles softly on Ryu's door.

Her gaze darted to the master suite at the end of the corridor.

A loaded silence echoed from inside Ryu's room. Mae scowled. She pressed her cheek to the door.

"*I know you're both in there!*" she whispered fiercely.

There was a thud, followed by a muffled curse. The door opened a fraction a few seconds later.

"Hmm, hi Mae," Ryu warbled, tugging her nightshirt down over her thighs.

"Keep it down!" Mae hushed her. She looked past

Ryu's shoulder to where Noah was hastily stepping into his jeans by her bed and narrowed her eyes at the sorcerer. "Seriously, dude, you're an animal. It's a miracle my sister can even walk."

Ryu flushed. Noah looked appropriately guilty.

"Anyway, why is Mr. Fusanaga in Mom's room?" Mae muttered.

Ryu blanched. "*Wait, what?!*"

"Oh." Noah grimaced at Ryu. "You didn't know?"

"No!" Ryu yelped.

"*Shh!*" Mae and Noah whispered frantically.

Mae froze when Ye-Seul's door opened. Her grandmother came out of her room and squinted at them before glancing at Yoo-Mi's room.

"Some people are getting all the action these days," she said morosely as she headed for the stairs. "I'll get breakfast started. And maybe make some calls to a dating agency. I bet Ilya knows some places."

I think your grandmother meant that, Brimstone told Mae solemnly as they all stared after her disappearing figure. *I don't think it's good for her to be indulging in that kind of activity at her age. She could break a hip, or worse.*

Mae shuddered.

The master suite opened. Yoo-Mi came out, Mr. Fusanaga behind her. Her eyes bulged when she saw Mae and Ryu. She turned, shoved Mr. Fusanaga back inside, and slammed the door closed in their faces.

"I hope you're using protection, young lady!" Ryu warned in the silence that followed. "Old lady! *Shoot!* Lady!"

"Oh God," Noah groaned.

Mae sagged. "It's too early for this."

She went back to her room, determined not to come out until she was at least fifty.

A week had passed since she'd returned from Europe. It had been even longer than that since the battle that had seen the headquarters of the Council of the Moon reduced to smithereens.

Dealing with the aftermath of their most recent clash with the Dark Council, including the Hellfire-Magic-induced earthquake that had damaged Prague, had taken its toll on Marlena while she'd dealt with the city officials and worried coven members who'd come knocking at her front door every day. Luckily, Ludmila had stuck around to help.

It was thanks to the Vissarion matriarch and Budimir's interventions that the Council of the Moon had not ended up incurring heavy fines or being kicked out of the city for good.

Mae had spent several days fixing Cortes's core while they'd rested at the Stanisic mansion. It had taken Nikolai helping her with his white magic for her to completely restore the Colombian's powers.

Instead of being grateful, the mobster had dragged them to every pet shop in Prague and several other cities on the continent in a bid to find himself a new familiar, a venture which had proven unsuccessful.

"I think you'll find a familiar closer to home," Mae had told him when they'd finally prepared to leave Paris to return to the States.

"You think so?" Cortes had said glumly.

"Yeah." Mae had patted him gently on the back. "I bet your familiar is going to be amazing."

The Colombian had given her a rare smile at that.

As for the Dark Council, Mae hadn't sensed their presence or Vedran's portal since that day. They were certain Oscar had told his father about Nikolai's ability to wield Hellfire Magic by now. The fact that there had yet to be any signs of movement by the Sorcerer King worried Mae.

What's he planning now?

She came out of her room midmorning, having showered and dressed. A faint commotion drew her to the window on the landing. Her eyes rounded.

A queue of SUVs with tinted glass was parked outside her mother's house.

"What the—?!"

I sense Tarang, Brimstone said. *And Alastair.*

Mae stormed down the stairs, the fox leaping the steps beside her. A brouhaha rose from the direction of the kitchen and the living room. She checked out the kitchen first.

"Oh hey, Mae," Milo mumbled around a cinnamon roll, hand lifting in a friendly wave.

Ilya dipped his head. "Good morning."

Mae drooled a little. Several boxes of *Vetriano's* breakfast pastries lay on the table. *Vetriano's* was the best Italian bakery in New York. For some reason, Vlad seemed to be at the top of their VIP list.

Ye-Seul served Ilya tea and eyed Mae with a faint frown. "I hope you and Ryu will be understanding toward your mother."

Mae squirmed awkwardly under her accusing stare. "I wasn't intending to tell her off." She chewed her lip. "How long have you known?"

"Since the beginning." Ye-Seul shrugged. "She's my daughter. I'd have to be a fool not to realize what was going on." She paused, her expression softening. "He's a good man, Mae."

"What's up?" Milo said curiously, his gaze swinging between them.

"My mom got a new beau," Mae muttered.

Milo choked on his roll. Ilya sighed and patted him forcefully on the back.

Mae studied the other guards seated in her mother's kitchen with a jaundiced air before heading to the living room. She stopped in the doorway, put her hands on her hips, and glared at the crowd packing the place.

"What in the ever-living hell are you goons doing in my house on a goddamn Sunday morning?!"

CHAPTER THIRTY-NINE

Bryony sniffed. "How rude."

Vlad greeted Mae with a smile that made her pulse skitter. "Good morning, Princess."

Brimstone headed over to Tarang, tail swinging.

"Hi, Mae," Nikolai said guiltily.

"I was coming home today," Mae told the sorcerer stiffly.

Cortes stared.

"Wait. They're living together?" he asked Vlad.

The Columbian was leaning next to a window with his arms crossed.

Vlad's smile faded. "It's a temporary arrangement."

Budimir bobbed his head solemnly where he sat on a couch. "Mae."

"Hi, Mae," Roman said shyly beside him.

"You're looking sprightly this morning, Witch Queen." Ludmila beamed. She scanned Mae from head to toe and glanced pointedly at Vlad. "My, aren't those some *fertile* hips you have there?"

Mae sucked in air.

Bryony sprayed out the mouthful of tea she'd just swallowed. Violet passed the coughing High Priestess a hanky.

"I thought we decided to leave that kind of trash talk back in Prague," Nikolai growled at Ludmila.

Ludmila arched an eyebrow. "You mean, *you* decided?"

"Now, now, children," Vlad drawled.

Yoo-Mi came into the room, a sheepish Mr. Fusanaga following in her wake.

"Hi, Bryony," Mae's mother said stiltedly. She greeted Nikolai, Vlad, and the Nolan cousins, and stared at the visitors she didn't recognize. "Are these new friends of yours?"

Mae swallowed a sigh at the way Yoo-Mi avoided her eyes. "Yeah." She peeked at Mr. Fusanaga. "And honestly, it's okay. Ryu isn't upset either. She was just a bit shocked."

Yoo-Mi flinched and finally met her gaze. Color returned to her face. "It just kinda…happened."

Mr. Fusanaga took her hand. The rest of the room stared.

"Might as well make it official." Yoo-Mi took a deep breath. "Everyone, I'd like to introduce you to Mr. Itou Fusanaga, my new, er, boyfriend."

Vlad's elbow slipped off his knee. Nikolai's cup crashed to the floor. Bryony's jaw dropped open. Miles swallowed a pastry the wrong way.

"Holy crap," Violet mumbled.

She slapped her choking cousin distractedly on the back.

Mr. Fusanaga's expression turned glassy as he found himself the focus of a battery of shocked and confused stares. "Hmm, hello."

"I'll go make some more tea," Yoo-Mi said, like she'd just spoken about the weather. "And get a mop and a dustpan for that."

She indicated the spillage by Nikolai's feet.

"I'll grab them!" The sorcerer jumped to his feet and dashed awkwardly out of the room.

Mr. Fusanaga followed him. "I'll help."

Yoo-Mi made to leave. She paused on the threshold of the living room, turned, and narrowed her eyes slightly at Mae. "By the way, do our new guests have anything to do with the incident in that city you went to? You know, the one that made the news?"

Mae squirmed under her probing stare. Her mother could read her like an open book. "Er, maybe?"

Yoo-Mi muttered something under her breath and left.

Silence ensued.

"What was that about?" Ludmila said.

Mae explained.

Ludmila's expression cleared. "Ah. I see. I've had five husbands myself."

"You say that like you're proud."

"I am," Ludmila grunted. "They were all filthy rich and," she leaned forward, her voice dropping to a theatrical whisper, "*well endowed.*"

Roman flushed. Budimir frowned.

Bryony's expression grew pinched. "Really, Ludmila."

"My Enrique is well endowed too," a voice said spiritedly.

Cortes flinched. Mae blinked. Her gaze found the Colombian's stony face before dropping to a covered birdcage by his feet.

She hadn't noticed it before.

Brimstone trotted over and sniffed the cover. *It's a familiar.*

Mae brightened. "You found a familiar?"

Cortes clenched his jaw. "He's on probation."

Vlad's shoulders trembled. Mae realized the incubus was trying not to burst out laughing. Her puzzled gaze swung to Cortes.

"Where did you meet him?" she said curiously.

"In a pet shop, in the Bronx," Nikolai muttered as he returned with a mop and a dustpan.

He gave Cortes a look of pity and cleaned up the broken cup and spilt tea.

"Oh." Mae looked from Nikolai to Vlad and Cortes, surprised. "I didn't know you guys were hanging out."

"We didn't have a choice in the matter," Nikolai said a tad coolly. "He practically forced us to go with him to every pet shop in the damn city."

Mae grimaced at the Colombian. "Seriously? That shit gets old fast."

Cortes didn't bat an eyelid.

"How about you introduce me to everyone?" the voice said brightly at his feet.

Cortes smiled brittlely. "Excuse me." He grabbed the

birdcage, parted an opening in the cover, and glared at whatever was inside. "How about you pipe down before I shoot you?!"

The unseen voice sniffed. "Tough words from a guy who couldn't properly access his magic until I showed him how."

"Is it a parrot?" Roman asked.

Filomena tasted the air curiously with her tongue where she perched on his head.

Cortes hesitated as he found himself the center of attention. He reluctantly uncovered the birdcage.

A Macaw with dazzling, red feathers and golden eyes peered out at them from behind the bars. He blinked when he saw Mae.

He whistled shrilly and started bobbing his head. "Hot babe alert! Hot babe alert!"

Mae gaped. A low growl escaped Brimstone.

Cortes looked like he wanted to sink into the ground.

The parrot checked Violet over with a tilt of his head. He navigated his perch and leaned close to his sorcerer.

"I mean, she's pretty too, Enrique, but her chest is a bit, you know, *flat*," he whispered.

Purple magic blossomed around Violet. Trixie bared her teeth.

"That thing has a death wish," Budimir muttered.

"I like his spirit," Ludmila asserted. "What's his name?"

Cortes assumed the appearance of a man about to kiss his reputation goodbye.

"—po," he mumbled.

Ludmila put a hand to her ear. "What?"

"It's Mister Popo," Cortes said between gritted teeth.

A strangled snort escaped Nikolai as he made to leave the room with the mop and dustpan. Tears were streaming down Vlad's face where he quaked with silent laughter. Mae bit her lip hard.

Cortes scowled at Nikolai and Vlad. "You assholes are dead."

"I've told you a dozen times already, Enrique," the parrot whined. "It's *Sir* Popo."

Cortes's dagger appeared in his hand.

The parrot gulped and stepped hastily to the far side of his cage. "Alright, how about the rest of these peons address me as Sir Popo and you and that hot lady over there just call me Popo?"

Vlad sobered. "Peons?"

The bird ignored the scowls being directed at him and cocked his head at Mae. "She can stroke my feathers all day long, you know what I me—?"

Cortes reached through the cage and clamped his beak shut.

"How about we swap familiars?" the Colombian told Vlad.

"Hell no!"

The incubus hugged Tarang.

Mae rolled her eyes as they started a heated exchange and looked inquisitively at Budimir and Ludmila. "By the way, what brings you two to the

States? I didn't know you were intending to visit so soon."

Budimir and Ludmila turned to Roman and gave him an encouraging smile. Mae stared, puzzled.

Roman rose and cleared his throat. "I—I would like to be considered as one of your potential consorts."

He blushed.

A shocked hush followed his words.

"Huh?" Mae said blankly.

"What?!" Nikolai snapped.

Vlad rose, a scowl darkening his face. "Why, this little punk!"

Miles clapped his hands. "*Oooh*, plot twist!"

Violet grinned and bit into a biscuit, her amused gaze swinging between Mae, the two sorcerers, and the incubus.

Roman's expression grew determined. "I don't feel that I'm lacking in any way compared to them." He shot a mutinous look at Vlad and Nikolai. "As for our age gap, Azazel and Ran Soyun's was a thousand times bigger. Besides, you've—" He faltered, his ears turning beet red. "You've already had my first kiss!"

Mae's jaw dropped open as gasps echoed around the room.

"You cradle snatcher!" Bryony whispered, aghast.

Nikolai and Vlad looked stunned enough to be knocked over by a feather.

Brimstone squinted at Mae. *How depraved, my witch. I did not know your inclinations ran that way.*

"It was a kiss of life, alright?!" she spluttered. "He was drowning!"

"Be that as it may, there is no denying that you have violated my great-grandson's lips, Witch Queen," Ludmila asserted sharply.

Budimir nodded, expression adamant. "He deserves a chance too."

Mae could tell they were serious about backing Roman's proposal.

She met the young sorcerer's resolute gaze. "I—"

Roman put up a hand and stopped her. "I'm not expecting you to give me an answer right now. I…just want you to consider it."

Mae chewed her lip.

"How about you take all four of them?" Mister Popo wheezed as he finally escaped Cortes's hold. "And by that, I mean my Enrique too, of course." The parrot eyed Nikolai, Vlad, and Roman beadily. "They all look pretty well endowed, but I have seen my Enrique in the shower and I can assure you that his peni—"

Yoo-Mi came in the room. "I'm making *Hoeddekk*. Who wants some?" She blinked at Mister Popo. "Oh. What a charming Macaw."

The parrot brightened and opened his beak. A strangled protest left him as a circle of threatening spell bombs surrounded his cage.

THE END

❋

Mae, Brimstone, and Hellreaver's adventures continue in Midnight Witch.

ACKNOWLEDGMENTS

To my friends and family. I couldn't do this without you.

To my readers. Thank you for reading Of Flames and Crows. If you enjoyed my book, please consider leaving a review on Goodreads or on the store where you purchased it. Reviews help readers like you find my books and I truly appreciate your honest opinions about my stories.

Make sure to sign up to my store newsletter for special deals on my books and new release alerts. Or you can sign up to my author newsletter to get upcoming release notifications, sneak peeks, and giveaways.

BOOKS BY A.D. STARRLING

SEVENTEEN NOVELS

Hunted

Warrior

Empire

Legacy

Origins

Destiny

SEVENTEEN SHORT STORIES

First Death

Dancing Blades

The Meeting

The Warrior Monk

The Hunger

The Bank Job

LEGION

Blood and Bones

Fire and Earth

Awakening

Forsaken

Hallowed Ground

Heir

Legion

WITCH QUEEN

The Darkest Night

Rites of Passage

Of Flames and Crows

Midnight Witch

A Fury of Shadows

Witch Queen

DIVISION EIGHT

Mission:Black

Mission: Armor

Mission:Anaconda

MISCELLANEOUS

Void - A Sci-fi Horror Short Story

The Other Side of the Wall - A Horror Short Story

ABOUT A.D. STARRLING

Visit AD Starrling's store at shop.adstarrling.com and buy her ebooks, paperbacks, hardbacks, special edition print books, and audiobooks direct

Want to know about AD Starrling's upcoming releases? Sign up to her author newsletter for new release alerts, sneak peeks, giveaways, and more

Follow AD Starrling on Amazon

Join AD's reader group on Facebook
The Seventeen Club

Check out this link to find out more about A.D. Starrling
Linktr.ee/AD_Starrling

Printed in Great Britain
by Amazon